# DEVIL AND DEITY

**V.J. Mathews**
Vanniyamparambil

**DEVIL AND DEITY**

**Novel**

(English Version of Malayalam novel "Mithya"

Published in 2015 by Kerala Sahithya Mandalam)

**Author**

**(Malayalam and English version)**

**V.J. Mathews Vanniyamparambil**

First published in 2019

| | | |
|---|---|---|
| Editing assistance | - | Mathew Jackson<br>P I Thampi,<br>GeorgePullat |
| Type set and Admin | - | Liji, Jobin |
| Cover design | - | Sumesh |



Published by: Amazon UK

Printed in Great Britain



ISBN: **978-93-5346-822-4**

**This book is dedicated to the fellow soldiers who lost their lives in 1971 Indo-Pak war.**

This is a work of fiction. Any resemblances to persons living or dead as to actual incident are purely coincidental. The war details are also imaginary



Price: - Rs. 300 /-

# DEVIL AND DEITY
**Novel**
**V.J. Mathews Vanniyamparambil**

**KERALA SAHITHYA MANDALAM**

---

61/615 Mrinal, Sreekandath Road, Ravipuram-
Kochi-682016
Phone- 9400436347

## When you turn the pages

## 1. A dare devil

Retired Indian Air Force pilot, Wing Commander V.D Enasu, AVSM, VM was known as a "Daredevil", when he was in service.

He was one among the heroes who led the Indian Armed Forces to win over Pakistan during the Indo - Pak conflict in 1971. If it wasn't for his extra ordinary courage to bombard 'Sargodha Airbase' of Pakistan, it would have been difficult for the Indian armed forces to achieve victory over Pakistan and fly the Indian tricolour high, after the war in 1971. The Nation, in recognition for his extraordinary courage, bravery and commitment, awarded and honoured him with AVSM medal (Athi Vishista Seva Medal), one of the gallantry awards for extraordinary bravery.

V D Enasu was nick named "Dare Devil" by his colleagues long before the war.

In 1962, young officer Enasu was holding the lower rank of "Flying Officer", and was stationed at Jorhat Air Force Camp.

He was ordered to fly to Dibrugarh in his 'Otter' aircraft to take some testing equipment along with three technicians. It was one-and-a-half-hour flight from Jorhat to Dibrugarh. Distance was about three hundred and fifty kilometers.

It was a DHC-3 Otter, a single engine, propeller driven, low flying utility aircraft with a carrying capacity of one-ton weight along with four passengers. Short duration air travel in a low flying small aircraft is always very pleasant, and Enasu enjoyed his duty as a pilot of Otter aircraft.

Flying from Jorhat to Dibrugarh was very pleasant. While returning, the take off from Dibrugarh was also very smooth. But after fifteen minutes of flying, while crossing the Naga Hills, the engine developed some problem and started to produce unusual sounds which made Enasu and passengers panic. Slowly, that sound increased and turned into a very high pitched roar, like a sten gun firing. Fut....... fut.........fut.......

Enasu got worried. He was helpless in mid air, above the dense forest. The passengers were petrified. They all were shivering and a young sergeant amongst the passengers started to yell. Suddenly, the aircraft engine stopped and the propeller became still. The plane started to descend with its nose down. Enasu had seen the dark of forest fast approaching towards him. The death bell started to ring in his ears. The airmen cried aloud frantically.

When the aircraft was just about to touch the tree top, to their surprise and relief, the engine started abruptly. The propeller whirled violently, which enabled the flight to lift itself up in full speed. It was a very narrow escape. All of them looked at each other in bewilderment.

"I guess we are ok. It could have been a fuel valve blockage or something like that. Any way we are safe now. All of you can relax", Enasu announced.

No one could respond. They were still under fright and shock. Their throats were dry and choked due to fear.

Further flying was smooth. The climate was also pleasant. The beauty of the terrain below was eye catching. But no one could enjoy the scenic beauty of nature as they were not free from their frightening experience.

The peace did not last long, as the engine started to cough again 'fut…fut…fut….!

This time the sound was louder than before and it was ear blasting. It sent shock waves down their spine.

The roar of the engine increased and the aircraft started to vibrate violently. Everybody was afraid that the plane would tear apart any moment. The engine became still again. The propeller stood motionless. Frantic cries and hysterical curses echoed in the cabin.

The plane looked down at forty-five-degree angle. The altitude was dropping rapidly. Enasu could see the Brahmaputhra river, which was fast approaching towards them as if to swallow the plane. He came face to face with death again. A dreadful death by drowning may be the destiny of these air warriors.! With shivering hands, Enasu gripped the joystick. He pressed the throttle with all his might and shouted aloud "Pull up, you bloody bastard bitch"!

Aircraft might have heard that frightened roar. With a violent jerk the engine started again. The propeller whirled. Aircraft looked up and pulled up to the sky with full speed. If the engine had failed to start that very moment, the plane would had plunged into the deep water of Brahmaputhra river.

Again, it was a lucky escape. The plane spiralled and surged up to the sky.

No one could utter a word of joy or sound a sigh of relief. All were startled. After a few minutes of further flying, Enasu could see the Jorhat runway fast approaching him, waiting to receive the plane.

Somehow he managed to land the plane at the centre of the runway. But the aircraft could not run more than forty yards. She skidded and turned ninety degrees starboard (right side) and stopped.

His flight was being monitored in the radar at the OPS Centre. They were shivering with fright when the 'Otter' plane dipped twice in mid air. And from that very day, Enasu was crowned with the nickname "Daredevil".

Further, his performances in the sky were in tune with his nickname. He was an adventurous and skilled pilot. There were three air mishaps in his career. Two ended up in 'belly landings'. Those landings exhibited the ultimate courage of Enasu. In both the cases, he saved himself and the aircrafts as well. But the third one was very serious.

The first air accident was in 1968, when he was in Halwara Air force squadron. It was a Gnat jet fighter. He was flying back to the base camp after a routine surveillance flight through the Pakistan border. At around six in the morning when he was trying to land his plane, the front wheel did not come out of the fuselage. He frantically reported the matter to Air Traffic Control. He was ordered to orbit around the airport, in the meantime technical experts contacted him and gave instructions to get the undercarriage down. But it didn't work. Finally, he was ordered to bail out. There was no other go, nothing could have been done.

To bail out from Gnat aircraft, he had to pull an ejection lever situated just over his head. Pilot along with his seat would be then thrown out of the aircraft. The plane would plunge down when its forward momentum ceases. When it falls down, either the plane would be scattered into pieces or it would explode and set ablaze. The Pilot would have a safe landing with the help of a parachute.

When Enasu was about to pull the ejection lever, he saw thickly populated villages within two kilometers around the air force camp. If he bailed out, the aircraft would crash in any one of the villages and explode for sure. The casualties would be very high. He could not think of being responsible for such a mishap. Enasu instructed ATC to position an 'open jeep' at the landing side of the runway at the centre line, facing towards the far end, immediately.

"What the hell are you talking Enasu! I don't understand. What do you mean by positioning a jeep on the runway?". The panicky ATC controller barked.

"I will land the plane on that jeep. Jeep will act as my front wheel "Enasu said very calmly.

"Are you crazy? You will get yourself killed!"

"Heavensake let me try please!... I can't allow my kite to crash down on the village. The casualties and damages caused by the crash will be devastating. I would rather go down with my kite".

"What ...? What...?" The controller stammered in panic and confusion.

"Please do it immediately...... Right now!" Enasu shouted and ordered through the radio telephone and switched off the phone.

The controller knew Enasu very well. the decision once taken by him will be firm and final. Emergency siren was blown loudly. Emergency signals were aired. All the inhabitants of the camp were rushed to the runway. Fire engines, Ambulances and rescue parties were lined up. An open jeep was parked at the landing point of the runway facing the far end and the driver ran away. All were glaring at the runway waiting for a catastrophe to take place, by the fast approaching aircraft. They were all going to witness a horrible crash landing right in front of them. None of them had seen an air crash before. Now that was going to happen right in front of their eyes. 'Let God save the crack fellow Enasu' they all prayed. They all knew it is suicidal.

But by God's grace, the landing was almost perfect, just on the top of the jeep, although it made a terrible sound. The back wheels of aircraft were steady. The aircraft pushed the jeep forward for about few hundred meters straight through the runway. Suddenly the jeep turned to port (left) side. The aircraft skidded and went out of runway and got stuck in the loose sand. It was nothing less than a miracle. Enasu saved the lives and properties of the villagers, along with his favorite kite. Rescue team, airman and officers rushed towards the aircraft. They lifted Enasu in their shoulders and danced. All were shouting with excitement, joy and also scolded him with affection and relief.......". Reckless...Daredevil."

In 1969, just 16 months after that incident Enasu made another crash landing which was far riskier than Halwara incident.

That happened in Amritsar Air force camp in the month of December at 6am when entire Punjab was shivering due to heavy winter. Enasu was returning from the routine surveillance flight through the border. When he was about to land, back wheels of the under carriages got stuck. With singlefront wheel, landing would be impossible. There were no other alternatives. ATC commanded him to bail out. Enasu with his sharp eyesight noticed a wide stretch of ploughed paddy field with mud and water that looked like a lagoon just a few meters after the runway. As it was early in the morning there were no one in the field. The field was deserted. Ploughed soil mixed with water formed perfect clay. Enasu did not hesitate. He swiftly landed his aircraft in the field without wheels. It was a perfect belly landing. The plane bounced three times like a dolphin dive in the sea and got stuck in the clay.

The two landings were recorded with golden letters in the history of Air force. Enasu received his first gallantry award VM (Vayu Sena Medal), for his merit in successfully accomplishing a belly landing.

His bold and brave attitude was inherited, whereas, the fearless daredevil personality was developed due to hatred and circumstances he had gone through in his personal life. It had a psychological impact in shaping his mind and his daredevil attitude.

## 2. Suspecious man

Enasu hailed from one of the richest feudal Christian familes named Vazhakala in Kakkanadukara Village, in the outskirts of Ernakulam, Kerala.

The legacy of "Vazhakala" family was blood stained and horrific. His father, Devassy the youngest son of a Landlord Mathai, was a very daring man. The natives were looking at him with mixed feeling of respect and fear. His father, Enasu's grandfather, Mathai was a feudal land lord, and he was a friend of Tripunithura King, His Highness Rama Varma.

It was said that the rubber plantation was introduced in Kerala by Mathai. He had brought one hundred bags of rubber seeds from Malaya (present

Malaysia) by ship. For a long time, he was working in Malaya as an estate superintendent. He germinated the seeds and planted them it in one hundred and fifty acres of barren land taken on lease from the king of Tripunithura. The land was located in the western slope of Kakkanadu hills, later known as Kakkanadukara. The entire plantation had become the sole property of Mathai by a decree of the king (patta).

His youngest son Devassy Vazhakkala, the father of Enasu, was married to Elisa daughter of a farmer from a middle class family at Udayamperur. Elisa was a beautiful girl and was a dancer. In those days, stage performers were not much accepted by the society but their skills were well praised. Most of the artists were labelled as immoral by the society. Elisa was very beautiful and her performances were extraordinary and skilled. Once she performed a dance in the Darbar hall of Thripunithura palace, in the presence of the king and his friends. Mathai Vazhakala was also invited and seated in the Durbar along with the Royal guests. Mathai liked Elisa. He publicly proposed for the girl to her father for his son Devassy. The marriage was fixed there itself. Elisa had studied dance in Rama Varma Dance School, Tripunithura.

Devassy was initially reluctant to marry a dancer. But his father Mathai strongly insisted him to marry her as, it was a prestige issue for him to keep up the word given to Elisa's father in front of the king. Devassy did not have the courage to disobey his father.

Soon after the marriage, Mathai sent his son Devassy and his bride Elisa to Malaya on their honeymoon trip in a ship. During that time, the activist movements led by communists had initiated agitation against feudalism, which had flared up throughout Kerala.

One night the landlord Mathai Vazhakkala was murdered by the activists. The news rocked Kerala. It was a brutal killing. All newspapers and political parties deplored the killing. Mathai's head was chopped off and hanged on a post by the side of the market road. A placard was fixed on the post and a slogan was written on the placard in red letters.

"Inquilab zindabad
Down- Down feudalism
Eradicate feudalism".

Three elder children of Mathai fled from Kakkanadukara, otherwise they would have been killed too.

Devassy the youngest son came to know of the brutal murder of his father, as soon as he landed in Cochin after his honeymoon trip to Malaya. Everybody advised him against going to Kakkanadukara, and to keep away from the activists and be safe, he was asked to go to his wife's house at Udayamperur. Devassy send his wife to her house in a taxi tonga and he went straight to Vazhakala Plantation. He saw hundreds of red flags in front of his house, and at the estate gate.

He called all the workers from the quarters through messengers and asked them to assemble in front of his father's office. When all of them about hundreds were assembled in front of the office, he stood on a box and addressed them loudly.

"Ladies and gentlemen, you are all the employees of Vazhakala Plantation, who live with the remuneration given by us. We never considered you as mere labourers. We have considered you as our brothers and sisters. You were paid more than what other estates are paying to their employees. You know that very well. Yet, someone amongst you have killed your employer, my beloved father. I heard that they are searching for me and my brothers too, to kill. Now I am right in front of you, unarmed. If the murderers are here in this group, please come forward and kill me. Otherwise, If I happened to find out my father's murders, upon God, I am declaring now, that I will kill them for sure".

It was a roar of a courageous man and an open challenge to the murderers.

His strong and stern voice conveyed a sense of fright among the people and they openly agreed to extend their full cooperation and support to the management.

Within two days Devassy found out the murderers. They were four of them. Three were from his plantation and one was the local party secretary Karunan. Karunan was his classmate, who was a recipient of financial helps from his father Mathai.

The very next day Devassy came to know that the murderers were sitting in the toddy shop along with other activists.

In those days' people from well to do families and landlords would never enter local toddy shops. Entering into the toddy shop itself was considered to be indignity to high class society. Toddy shops were meant for laborers and lower class people.

The Landlord's son Devassy's sudden appearance at the toddy shop, shocked everyone seated inside.

Everyone in the shop stood up, as to show their respect to Devassy. With lightning speed, Devassy took out a sharp long blade hidden underneath his shirt, and charged towards the four murderers sitting around the table, drinking toddy and their heads were chopped off even before they could get up from their seats. Everything took place in a matter of seconds, their headless bodies were lying on the floor, and made a pool of blood all over the place. Devassy's white shirt was drenched in blood. There was a wild frantic hauling and loud hue and cry inside the toddy shop. Everyone including the shop owner ran out of the shop in panic.

Devassy went straight to the police station and surrendered himself. He handed over the blood stained blade and a huge packet of money to the police inspector who was his friend. Everyone expected death sentence for Devassy. If not, a life time imprisonment. Money had a high influence on judiciary during that period. After a short trial Devassy was sentenced for two years' imprisonment. His wife Elisa had stayed at her house at Udayamperur and continued with her dance practice, till Devassy came out of jail.

Devassy's life would have been wonderful, if he had not allowed suspicion to take over his mind. "A suspicious mind is a den of devils". One could have doubt but never suspicion. Suspicious mind would never find truth. It always misguides the soul and ruins your life. If you let suspicion in through one door, peace of mind would get away through the other. They never stay together. This is what happened in Devassy's life. After coming out of jail, Devassy brought his wife Elisa from her house to stay with him in Vazhakala bungalow. She became pregnant very shortly. The pregnancy took a toll on her, and she was suffering from vomiting, nausea, tiredness etc. She became pale and feeble. Her parents took her to their house at Udayamperur, so that her mother could provide better pregnancy care. She prematurely delivered a baby boy in the eighth month of her pregnancy. And thus Enasu, the protagonist was born. But soon suspicion and unwanted thoughts started creeping into Devassy's mind. Though premature delivery was not that unusual, he believed that the weight of the child would be significantly less when prematurely born. But Enasu's weight was two and a half kilograms which was very normal. Also, mothers who deliver prematurely would be bed bound for at least two months before they regain their health. But Elisa was seen very energetic and healthy. All these thoughts led Enasu's father to believe that he had been cheated by Elisa and that she was hiding something about her pregnancy. He suddenly thought of Udayan, Elisa's neighbour at Udayamperur. He was also a dancer and looked very feminine. Udayan was appointed in Vazhakala Estate office as a clerk by Devassy's elder brother Anthony while he was in jail. He came to know that Udayan was appointed due to pressure from Elisa. She and Udayan had jointly performed a couple of dance programmes in their church function. He also came to know that there were bad rumours about the duo prior to the marriage.

There were two more characters in Vazhakala Bunglow. They were Pappy and Kathry. Kathry was a spinster with a deformity in her leg. One of her legs was gaunted by polio. However, she was healthy and a good cook. She was the younger sister of Pappy.

Pappy was older than Anthony, the elder brother of Devassy, and was the personal servant of their father Mathai Vazakala till his death. He was a silent witness of all the happenings in the family. He was known as the conscience keeper of everybody at Vazhakala Bungalow, and everybody had confidence in him, as he was faithful.

When Enasu was five months old, Elisa and the baby were brought to Vazhakala Bungalow. Once when Udayan paid a visit to Vazhakal Bungalow to see the child, Devassy was not at home. When Devassy returned home he saw Udayan was sitting in his bed room holding the child in his hand and cuddling him. Elisa was sitting near him, placing a hand over his shoulder. Both seemed very happy in each other's company. Devassy did not like what he had seen. He asked Udayan in a very rude manner to go away. That hurt Elisa. Infant Enasu, extended both his tiny arms towards Devassy and smiled. He lifted the baby and held him tightly to his chest. When he touched the baby's chubby cheeks in a playful manner the baby started laughing loudly.

"When he laughs, he looks very cute" Pappy who was standing at the door commented.

"But I have seen the same type of smile on that Udayan's face too." Devassy said as insinuation with a mocking smile.

Pappy did not understand what Devassy meant by that comment. But Elisa understood. Her face fell and eyes were filled with tears.

The very next day morning, Udayan's dead body was found floating in Kakkanadu river, was flowing through the boundary of the Vazhakala plantation. He was wearing only his undercloths. His dress was kept folded at the bathing ghats a few yards away. A soap dish was also found by the side.

The news of the death of Udayan terrified Elisa. She felt that it was a homicide by Devassy, who had no reluctance in killing. She knew that Devassy did not like Udayan being close with her.

The next day morning, when he opened the bible for his routine reading he noticed something was scribbled on the first page of the Bible. That page was folded at the corner as a marker. Devasy read the scribbling. "Suspicious man is a devil. Only a devil can kill innocent people. I know you killed Udayan. It is very difficult for me to live with a suspicious husband. Please don't kill our child."

After a while Elisa's body was found floating in the fifty feet deep well behind the Vazhakkala Bengalow.

## 3. The back story

The untimely accidental demise of Elisa, left everyone in Vazhakkala family and the people of Kakkanadukara devastated. Everyone who knew Elisa endeared her for her charming personality. Apart from being a beautiful lady and a talented dancer, Elisa was humble, down to earth and polite towards everyone including poor labourers. This particular quality of Elisa made her stand out from other ladies of Vazhakala, who unlike Elisa, were reserved and hostile towards the poor people. It is being said that Elisa was sitting on the amillo (ring wall protecting a hand dug well) of the well talking to Kathry, the cook, when suddenly, she lost her balance and fell backward into the well head down. No one could help and save her life. "A cruel fate of destiny!"

The villagers carried on with the story narrated by Vazhakala Devassy, but felt sorry for her.

That evening Devassy was called to the police station by his friend, Inspector Ram. He showed Devassy, the postmortem report of Udayan. According to the report, though the deceased had mustache and hair on his chest, he did not have testicles and the male organ. He was a transgender female. Devassy was shell-shocked on hearing this.

Devassy was burdened with guilty conscience. He had committed a heinous crime. Out of remorse and despair Devassy decided to end his life just like Elisa. As soon as he reached home, he headed straight to his bedroom, frantically consumed half a bottle of whisky, and ran towards the well near the kitchen. He stepped on to the outer ring of the well and was about to jump. Suddenly, someone caught hold of his cloth from behind and pulled him back with great force. Devassy fell backward on the ground hitting his head hard on a stone. The fall was fierce. The fall knocked him unconscious and his head was bleeding profusely. Nobody was at home. All were at the funeral of Elisa. It was Kathry, the cook who pulled him back and saved his life. Though her left leg was handicapped due to polio, she was a stout woman with great strength and vigor. She lifted Devassy from the ground and carried him on her shoulders, and laid him on her bed in the servants' room near the kitchen. She washed his head with brandy, put some coffee powder on the cut and bandaged it with cloth torn out from her saree.

When Devassy gained consciousness, he tried to get up. But Kathry made him lie down and rested his head on her bulky lap. Devassy sobbed silently for a long time and slept.

Devassy and his brothers were living separately after the partition of their ancestral property. When partition among siblings were made, Devassy was entitled with the ancestral house and one fourth of Vazhakala Plantation with an extend of thirty acres. In that large ancestral house, only Devassy, his son Enasu, Pappy the senior servant and his sister Kathry resided.

Devassy brought up Enasu, with the help of Kathry in the absence of Elisa. Enasu was provided and cared for all his needs by Devassy. Devassy tried to compensate Elisa's absence by providing Enasu with all luxuries in life. Devassy felt remorseful for doubting his wife and for suspecting the paternity of his own son.

When Enasu was studying in college, his college mate who happened to be from Udayamperur and a distant relative of Elisa, told him about the rumor being told by everyone regarding the death of Elisa. It is being said that, the death of Elisa was not accidental and that it was a homicide and that the murderer was his father Devassy.

"How do you know"? Enasu was horrified.

"It is an open secret in our family circle", the gossiper said.

Although Enasu knew what he heard was not true, his mind was disturbed. So, he went to Pappy, the loyal servant of the family, and asked him regarding the death of his mother Elisa.

"Pappy Chetta (brother)", do you remember how my mother Elisa died?

"Oh, you were only six months old then".

"How did she die? Was it an accident or a murder"?

Pappy was shocked and appalled by what he had heard.

"What nonsense are you talking my son.? Who told you this"?

Enasu explained to him, what he had heard from his college mate.

"My dear boy, that is only a rumour. It was neither an accident nor a murder. It was a suicide", the old man said.

"Suicide? Do you mean my mother had committed suicide"? Enasu asked him in bewilderment.

"You don't believe me? I will show you the evidence".

The old man Pappy went to the bed room of Devassy and took out the old Bible kept on the bed side table. He opened it, and showed Enasu the scribbling Elisa made on it. The hand written letters on the page had faded but it was readable. He read it, and secretly took out the page and put it in his pocket.

"That was the suicide note written by Lady Elisa"

"Why did she commit suicide?

Oh my son. It happened about nineteen years ago. Please forget it".

"No Pappy Chetta, I want to know about it. I am entitled to know about the truth behind my mother's death". Enasu insisted.

"Your mother lady Elisa was a good dancer. Udayan, who was also a dancer and clerk at our factory office was your mother's neighbour. Both of them used to perform together on stage in public functions before to her marriage. Your father Devassy was suspicious of their relationship and confronted about it with your mother. When questioned, Lady Elisa got offended. There was a heated argument between your father and mother. Out of fury, your father told her that, he doubted their relationship and was suspicious of the paternity of their child. It was a provocative statement made by Devassy. Elisa felt very bad as her integrity and faithfulness in marriage was being questioned by her own husband. It was too much for her to handle.

Hey my son, please don't brood over in this matter, as it had happened long ago and nothing can be done about it;" Pappy said.

But, Enasu could not get over this. He went into deep thoughts, He had to find answers to a lot of questions. Why had father suspected my paternity? Was there any fact in it? If so, father would not have given me so much of love and care. He loves me so much. Without any solid reason father would not have killed that dancer Udayan. Why did she write, "Please don't kill our child"? What did she mean by the word "Our"? The word "child" denotes me. But, who is she referring to as "our"? Was it Udayan and mother or father and mother". Does my father still doubt my paternity? Am I really a bastard? He was confused and overwhelmed with a lot of questions. Enasu was extremely upset and in a state of confusion and shock. He headed to the well and glared into it, where his mother had commited suicide.

Enasu's mind was in a state of despair. He didn't know whom to blame in this matter, was it his father's fault? or was it his mother or Udayan who is to be blamed? Was it fate? A strange sense of hatred filled his mind, he loathed everyone and everything including himself. He was in a state of despair, he wanted to get away from everyone and everything. He wanted to get away from all his personal grievances.

Fortunately, a campus recruitment was conducted in the college to select people to become Air Force Pilots. Enasu got recruited and was fortunate enough to wear the Indian Air Force uniform.

Enasu's psyche was deeply influenced by his past. Everything that he faced and experienced in life was converted and channelled into a sense of courage and moulded him into a bold and daring man, thus, eventually earning him the nickname, "Daredevil".

## 4.Rendezvous

For three consecutive years Enasu did not avail his annual leave. He was entitled 45 to 60 days to vacation, as per service rules and duty situation. During emergencies, the commanding officer, if found deemed necessary, has the discriminative power to cancel the leave at anytime. Apparently, Enasu never bothered to go home.

It was not that he did not love his father and his house. He loved him and he was sure that his father loved him too. They were so close that, till adolescence he slept in the warmth of his father's hairy chest. That warmth and comfort provided by his father was more like a lullaby that soothed him to sleep. His father meant everything to him and was more valuable than anything else in the world. Yet a slight feeling of animosity developed in him towards his father, who was responsible for his mother's death. That thought made him flee from his beloved father and home. When he was alone, he always pondered about his father and the wonderful moments they had. The thought of his father brought tears in his eyes and a strong urge to see him.

One day when he was at Delhi Palam station, resting in pilot's waiting room, after a routine practicing flight, he was called up by his commanding officer to his office. Enasu got tensed. What could be the reason? Has something gone wrong? He was anxious to know the reason for being summoned by the C.O.

When Enasu reported to C. O's office, he was not available there. The Adjutant directed him to Officer's mess.

"He is waiting for you... You have a guest... C.O. is with him".

The arrogant adjutant did not bother to tell him who the guest was. He did not enquire about the guest either. Enasu felt that it would be better to refrain from further conversation with the short tempered officer. He ran to the Officer's mess eagerly and was shocked to find his father Devassy sitting with his commanding officer, sipping tea.

"Hey Enasu, your father would be the first person in the history of my service, to come all the way from Kerala to Delhi to pick up his son to take him home. It is more like a mother picking up her child from nursery school." The Commanding Officer commented and laughed.

Devassy ran to his son, embraced him and asked "Did you forget me, my dear son"?

Enasu became overwhelmed by the heartfelt words, from his father. He also embraced his loving father and sobbed...The C.O. was watching them with a smile.

The C.O. asked Enasu, "Enasu, why haven't you availed your annual leave for the past two years? This year also you have not applied for leave, Why"? Enasu was silent.

"Look Enasu you are lucky to have such a loving and caring father. You are everything to him. Here after, don't let him sob like this. He brought you up without a mother. He never even bothered to think about a second marriage and that was solely for you...young man.... Go along with him today itself.

I am granting you, sixty days leave. There is a mail flight at six in the evening via Nagpur and Madras to Cochin. I will book tickets for you… OK?... The ticket fare will be debited from your account of course." It was C.O.'s order.

The father and son travelled together by Indian Airlines night flight and reached home.

During lunch time Devassy asked his son. "Why did you avoid coming home to meet your father all these years? What was the constraint? Did I hurt you in any way? You are my life and hope. I live for you. I never made you cry for anything. I love you so much. Still…."

Devassy could not control himself and wept. It was heartbreaking to see his father cry, as he had never seen his father cry ever before. For him, his father was the strongest hearted, daring and courageous man, who had the courage to kill four miscreants with a sword by chopping off their heads single handedly.

"Appa (means father), please forgive me! Please don't cry! I can't bear…. I can't bear to watch you like this… please Appa."

Enasu also wept. The frustration and a bit of animosity Enasu had aganist his father melted away as tears. He hugged his father and kissed his cheek like a child and forgave his father.

That night, when they were having their dinner, Enasu said to his father. "Appa, it may sound silly, but, I am deeply disturbed by the sight of that well in which my mother died. Why don't we dig another well and cover this one? We must get rid of that devilish well. It always reminds me of her death".

Devassy became very uneasy. "My son, you are grown up and you are a brave soldier, that too a pilot. Your commanding officer told me that you are very brave. Then why are you afraid of a well in which an accidental death had occurred. Don't believe in bad spirit and demon. There are no such things".

"No Appa. It is not that I am afraid of spirit and devil. The sight of the well reminds me of so many things. Somebody told me my mother's death was an accident. Whereas others told me it was a suicide. I also heard a rumour that she was brutally murdered."

Devassy was surprised and shocked. He never knew that his son was aware of the gossips being circulated by people, about an incident that had happened when he was only six months of age.

"Son, all those are rumours. It happened long ago, when you were an infant. Rumours spread like wildfire, please don't ruminate on this matter". Devassy wanted him to skip the topic.

"No Appa. I want to know whether my mother had committed suicide or was killed. I have a scribbled note written by her. It's either a suicide note or she was killed because she had written that note".

"What note?'

"The one which was on the first page of the old bible, kept on your bedside table".

"Oh .... you have seen that?" Devassy asked in astonishment.

"I had stolen the page three years ago and I keep it with me since".

"For what?"

"I don't know Appa... I wanted to keep it. It was the last few lines written by my mother. Each word in that scribbled note, will have a story to tell... There are a lot of stories that I am unaware of. But, you could help to clarify all the unanswered questions in my mind. This would help me, to be at peace with my past. It is my right to know the truth about my mother's past", Enasu said firmly.

Devassy looked at him for some time.

"Do you want me to go away?" asked Pappy, who was serving dinner at the dining table and he was about to leave.

Suddenly Devassy said "No Pappy, please stay! I want you to hear the full story too. I know, you knew some of it but......."

Devassy was silent for some time, then with a deep sigh said, "it is verydevastating for a man to have a lesbian lady as his wife and it is more painful to tell this to his son." Devassy's voice was quivering as he said this.

It was indeed very shocking for Enasu. "What are you saying Appa"? Enasu exclaimed. He could not believe his own ears.

"Yes, it is true my son...Oh... my God! how can I tell all those painful stories to my own son......." Devassy lamented.

"Don't feel bad Appa. Now, I understand what a turmoil you were going through. I am with you

Appa. Please tell me what had really happened?" Enasu pleaded.

"My marriage was fixed by my father without my consent. He was a very strict and adamant man. He had seen Elisa, dancing in king's palace at Tripunithura, in front of elite guests. He liked her and wished to make her, his daughter in law. He never bothered to ask me about it. Rather, he wanted me to obey him like an obedient servant. I was compelled to oblige to father's decision. I saw Elisa for the first time on the day of our betrothal at Church. On seeing her for the very first time, I was dumbstruck. I felt I was the luckiest man in the world to get a beautiful and charming lady as my wife. She was so beautiful and perfect that I couldn't ask for anything more. Deep down, I thanked and praised my father's decision. But during that period, someone secretly told me that, Elisa had a lover named Udayan, an Ezhava youth, who was also her neighbour. And that, he was also a dancer. I Didn't take it seriously and dismissed it as a silly rumour. I hated Udayan at the very first glance. He looked feminine but never knew, he was a transgender female until I saw his postmortem report".

Enasu was very much moved by his father's story. Devassy's eyes moistened, teardrops trickled down his cheeks. Pappy covered his mouth with both his hands and sobbed silently.

"Pappy Chetta, you may please take your seat", Enasu pointed at a chair in front of him.

"No my son. Thank you for your kind gesture, God bless you! I prefer to stand here" Pappy said with humbly.

"Pappy, you may please sit down". Devassy insisted. He sat on the edge of a chair very reluctantly.

Deavassy continued, "Elisa was aloof in our bedroom which hurt me as a husband. Later I came to know it was because, she was a lesbian and due to the relationship that she shared with Udayan, that she was being indifferent. They were in a physical relation long before, she married me. Anyway, soon she conceived you and had a premature delivery the eighth month. I suspected that she had cheated me, till I saw the postmortem report of Udayan.

His death was indeed an accident. But Elisa thought that I had killed him. The unexpected demise of her lesbian partner was unbearable for her".

Devassy ended his story. He felt relieved from all the mental burden he carried all these years. He looked at Enasu and smiled. "Now read your mother's scribbled letter. Everything will be clear to you" Devassy said.

Enasu got up from his seat, went to his Appa and hugged him and said.

"Appa...you are great.... really great! I love you Appa."

# 5. The naughty girl

Enasu married Jainamma on 1'[t] March 1971. She belonged to Kottackal family hailing from Nellikkunnu, near Kothamangalam. She was the daughter of Raphel, a rich widower.

KottakkaI ancestral family bungalow was one of the famous heritage building in that region, constructed about 150 years ago. It was enormously big with so many rooms and amenities.

Raphel had identical twin daughters named Jainamma and Elamma. Both of them were stunning and enticingly beautiful. This made them extremely popular among young men in that area. Men dreamt of being in love with them and being in a relationship with them. Even a glimpse of them awed them.

Both the girls were five feet five inches tall, they had fair complexion with thick long curly hair. Their faces were plump with beautiful enchanting eyes with long lashes. They had long nose and beautiful red rose-petal like lips. They were so identical that it looked, as if God the great creator, sculptured and moulded them from a single mould.

Although they looked identical, their personalities were entirely different. Jainamma was an introvert whereas, Elamma was an extrovert. Jainamma was calm and composed. She was more intellectual, she enjoyed reading but Elamma was very active and energetic, she was fond of sports. She was a record holder in high jump, her favourite sport and also, was the captain of her college volleyball team.

Long ago, when Elamma was in college, she shocked the entire stadium with her dashing and daring performance wearing a tight short. In those days, people were extremely conservative. Women exposing their legs were considered as a sin. Women were expected to be fully clothed and modest. But

Elamma's daring performance in her shorts made the youngsters thrilled with amusement.

The parish priest, who was also the principal of the college, shouted at Elamma and ordered her to go out of the court and change the costume. She rushed to the changing room and reappeared wearing short skirt.

"You should have worn a pyjama" the priest said in resentment.

"Don't have one now." She said loudly.

Since there was ear blasting applauses of approval from the spectators the priest allowed her to participate in the tournament. But, she deliberately made her skirt to fly up, whenever she jumped high for smashing the ball over the net. This performance resulted in wild cheer and uproar among the spectators.

Her team had won the match. When the press photographers called her for taking snap photos, she rushed to the changing room and quickly re-appeared in her tight shorts. Photo of her wearing shorts, carrying a ball in her hand appeared in the sports column of all newspapers.

That was Elamma, the daring and mischievous girl. The parish priest considered her action, as a contemptible one. He complained about it to Raphel. He was infuriated upon hearing this from the parish priest. Out of fury and rage, Raphel thrashed Elamma for the first time in his life. But later Raphel felt sorry for thrashing his dear daughter and he himself applied ointment on the blood stained sores on her thighs and arms. Raphel, the loving father, could not control his emotions and started sobbing. This made the entire family sad and gloomy for days.

Elamma completed her B.sc nursing and applied for a job as military nurse. She was selected in a campus interview.

Raphel did not want his daughter to go for nursing.

"Why do you want to seek an employment? God has given us sufficient wealth to live for generation. I want you to get married and settle here."

He disliked her decision to take up the nursing job.

But Elamma was adamant, she cried and fought with her father till he had agreed.

Jainamma completed her B. Ed Examination. Even before the results were declared, she was appointed as a lecturer in a native college.

After two years since she left for work, Elamma came home for a month's leave, on March 15th 1971. Her annual leave entitlement was two months, however she decided to split her leave and avail the next leave in December. So that, she could attend the parish feast on December eighth and attend the Christmas on December twenty fifth.

In the meantime, Raphel made all arrangements for her marriage, through a broker. The broker successfully found an apt groom for Elamma. At the very first glance of the groom's photo, Raphel was convinced that he was the right match for his daughter. The family background was also acceptable to him.

The groom was Enasu. He was also on leave and in search of a girl to marry.

"If everything goes well, the engagement and marriage will be conducted simultaneously" Raphel told Jainamma.

"Will the church agree?" She enquired.

"We have to take permission from the Bishop. I will take care of that, no worries" said Raphel.

"I don't want to get married now. I want to work for two more years." Elamma told Jainamma secretly. She was afraid to talk about it to her father. She knew very well, how her father would react.

"Why Elamma...Why do you want to wait for so long?" Jainamma asked.

"If I marry now, I will lose my job. Military nurses are to be spinsters."

"Oh... they need not be virgin?"

"Don't joke. I am not bluffing... I don't want to get married so soon."

"Getting married is not a bad idea. Anyway, one day you have to get married. Then, why don't you do it now? Earlier the better." said Jainanna.

"Then you marry now. I will marry later. you are elder to me by fifteen minutes. That's what Mummy said". Elamma said.

"I am always ready. If papa asks me, I will surely agree".

"Ready.?"

"Why not?"

"Then why don't you tell papa……. You can save me as well."

"Why should I…... Pappa selected this guy for you……. He is a pilot. A very good alliance. An Air Force pilot is marrying a military nurse.' How wonderful".

"But I can't marry now…. Jainamma. I can't".

Elamma said very firmly.

"Why not?"

"I am in love with another man. …. He promised me, that he would marry me after two years, soon after his sister's marriage. It's fair, isn't it?"

Jainamma was shocked on hearing this. How can she talk like this? Father taught us well, he expects us to refrain from being in love and romance but Elamma's attitude was unacceptable and wrong.

"Elamma, you shouldn't have got yourself into such a precarious entangle. You will regret it later.

Please forget about it and agree to this marriage. This man is very handsome, and with authoritative look in his eyes. He is very special Elamma. Girls will envy you, if they see him.

"You have not seen him?" Elamma asked.

"I have seen his photo, Pappa showed it to me."

"Then you marry that enviable handsome man. I only want my Roy. I love him and he loves me." Then, she lowered her voice and whispered "We had sex together.... Now we can't be separated."

Jainamma was shocked. A sudden chill went through her spine. She was aghast and felt as if, the entire world was whirling around her. She tightly held the headrest of the chair and sat on it in dismay. She could not look at her sister's face. A sense of hatred was felt, towards her sister.

However, Jainamma presented the case to her pappa.

"Pappa.... Elamma says, she doesn't want to marry now. She wants to work for two more years."

Raphel was enraged and shouted... "Elamma. Come here!"

Elamma showed her frightened face from behind the door curtain.

"For God's sake tell me, why you are not willing to get married now.? Are you planning to join a convent and become a nun? I don't agree with that either. "He asked her in a raised voice with lot of discontent.

"I want to continue my job for two more years pappa. I like my job"... she pleaded.

"Bullshit. What nursing? Is it a good job? What do you earn from this job? Maximum thousand bucks a month? Is it a remuneration? My servant earns more than you. I will give you five thousand rupees as pocket money every month till your death." He roared like a lion.

Elamma just stood behind the door curtain, her head down.

"Now you listen!!" Raphel raised his voice again... "Once I decide on something, it should be done. Understood? Tomorrow, Vazhakala Devasy and his family members will come along with the groom Enasu to see you. If they like you, I will fix your marriage. Is it clear?"

Suddenly, Jainamma guided Elamma to their room.

Vazhakala party arrived just in time. They came in three cars. Jainamma was at the door step to receive the guests.

"Hey Raphel, is she the proposed girl?" Vazhakala Devassy asked in astonishment.

Usually, prospective bride will appear before the groom only when called. This was the custom that prevailed then.

"No... No... No, this is Jainamma. Sister of the proposed girl. Other girl is Elamma. They are twins." Raphel said.

Elamma appeared and served tea to the guests. Everyone liked the girl. A nod of approval was exchanged between the elders. Which was followed by customary talks on various subjects. Finally, they decided to fix the marriage date soon after the prospective bride and groom meet each other and give their consent. That was the custom.

Enasu was guided to the study room where Elamma was waiting for Enasu.

Elamma got up from the chair and requested Enasu to sit. "Please take your seat "he said... She sat down.

"You are Elamma, and the other girl is your twin sister Jainamma, right?"

"Yes you are right." She said with a smile.

"You both look alike. How do we distinguish both of you? I am confused" Enasu laughed.

"That is not an issue. Do you like us?" Elamma asked bluntly.

"Yes...Yes.... Why not. I like both of you. To be frank, both of you are very good looking girls. No doubt." He said smilingly

"But you can't marry both of us. Since we are not muslims to have two, three wives at a time." She giggled.

Enasu laughed, he liked Elamma's frankness. "That's right." He agreed.

"In that case, why don't you marry Jainamma. In Fact, she is more modest and she suits you better."

Enasu was stunned.!

"What are you talking? Elamma is my prospective bride...isn't it?" He asked.

"That's right. But, I have to tell you something serious, regarding this marriage proposal."

"What problem?"

"Please promise me that, you will not cheat me, if I disclose it to you."

"What do you mean?"

"Will you promise me that you will not reveal it to anyone?... Will you keep this as a secret?" She looked at his eyes directly. Her eyes were piercing.

"Yes"

"Promise", She stretched her right palm.

When Enasu placed his palm on her palm, she pressed his palm and held it tight. The softness of her palm sent chillwave through his nerves. Suddenly, he withdrew his hand and thought how naughty she was.

"I know what you are going to tell" Enasu said. You want to continue your job. If you get married you may lose your job, isn't it?" He asked.

"Oh...no..not that, I am in love with another person. He is a doctor in our hospital. Captain Roy. We have decided to marry."

He appreciated her frankness and boldness.

"What do you want me to do? He asked.

"In front of everyone, please tell my father that you don't like me but you are willing to marry Jainamma."

"If they ask the reasons?",

"Say something... Tell them that, you don't like nursing profession."

When Enasu openly said as, told by Elamma, Raphel got annoyed and offended.

"Didn't the broker tell you that, Elamma is a nurse and working in Delhi?" Raphel raised his voice and questioned Enasu.

"He did not tell me that she is a nurse. I don't like nursing profession." He said.

"Neither do I. She went for nursing on her compulsion. I did not like it. But what to do. She was adamant. Anyway that's all over. After the marriage she will not go for that job."

"I am interested in Jainamma." Enasu said categorically.

Elamma suddenly appeared from behind the door curtain and said boldly.

"Pappa...please don't get annoyed. It is destiny and I feel it is the divine ordination. . In fact, I don't want to get married now. I have written an exam for promotion. I selected this profession because of my passion and commitment and not for money. It is for my mental satisfaction. Give me two more years.

Jainamma has no objection towards this proposal. Why don't we give her to Enasu?"

All were looking at her with astonishment and admiration. Raphel was compelled to agree.

Enasu married Jainamma on 1st March 1971.

## 6. A grieved father

The hasty marriage was an unexpected surprise and a God given gift for Jainamma. She never thought of her marriage till, her name was publically proposed by Enasu. She was awed at what just happened. What she told Elamma about her willingness for marriage was a mere joke but it turned out to be a reality. The circumstances guided Jainamma to the wedding alter. It was destiny.

Raphel became very upset. He had no other option than to accept Enasu's proposal. The pressure tactics of Elamma became successful.

But the calculation made by Raphel went astray. He had definite plans for his daughters. Elamma had to be married first, so that she would get rid of her nursing job. She should be handed over to a strong hand who is strong enough to fix up a bridle on her. If guided well, Elamma would be an efficient housewife. If let loose, she would become a mad stallion.

He always wanted Jainamma to be in his vicinity. He planned to get her married to a boy who could be adopted into the family, preferably from the native, if possible from the neighborhood. He had somebody in his mind. He wanted his son-in-law to be always at Kottakal to take care of his property. But God had other plans.

Elamma was very proactive in organizing the marriage of Jainamma. She herself contacted event management teams to make arrangements for the construction of 'reception pavilion' along with its interior decoration and so on.

She decided the menu for the feast and confirmed the order with cateress. She made the list of invitees and personally invited them on behalf of the family. She had done everything by herself. Raphel had to just give her a nod of approval on all her suggestions, and her suggestions were very apt and proper.

After the wedding ceremony she stood with garlands in her hands at the entrance of the house to receive the bride and bridegroom. That was the privilege of the head female member of the family preferably, mother, and that was the custom.

Everything went on well. Well organized and preplanned. Invitees had a lot of praise for her and commented "Raphel is a lucky man to have a daughter like Elamma. Although, she is a woman, she is as competent and capable as a man."

After the feast, all the invitees went back and it was time to bid farewell to her father. The first night of the newly wedded couple would be at groom's house. That was the custom.

Raphel could not hold back his tears, when Jainamma embraced him to bid farewell. She was also weeping at that time. Elamma consoled both of them, as if she was an experienced aged lady.

"When will you be going back to Ambala?" Raphel asked Enasu. "I have forty days leave left pappa." Enasu said.

"Will you visit this old man before you go back." Raphel's eyes were moist and words were broken as spoke.

"Oh....My ...God ...oh...pappa.... what is this!" Enasu was overwhelmed. "We will be coming every weekend to stay with you for two or three days. Vazhakkala is not that far away. Only one-hour drive, not a big issue."

His reply made Raphel very happy and Elamma became very joyous.

As promised, Enasu visited Kottackal every weekend with Jainamma and stayed in his wife's house for two to three days ... during each visit.

At Vazhakkala, Devassy was overjoyed by the arrival of his daughter- in-law Jainamma to his house. He wanted Jainamma to take over the entire affairs of his family. He had placed the key bunch of all the lockers in Vazhakkala house in front of Jainamma and said "Look my dear, Enasu is my only son and heir of all my wealth. Now onwards you will be the custodian of our lockers."

"Oh...Appa...I have to leave this house along with Enasu to his workplace, Ambala, after a month." Jainamma said helplessly.

"Hey Enasu, my son, why don't you discontinue your pilot's job and settle down at your own house. Now you are a married man and you have to rear your children in this house." The father spoke from his heart.

"Oh, Appa, give me two more years. By the time I will complete my initial contract period with Air force. Then I will leave Air force and live with you in this house permanently. That is a promise." He said sincerely.
But he could not fulfill his promises. His fate was different. Very different.

It was Enasu's second weekend visit to his wife's house. After an extravagant and lavish dinner, Jainamma guided Elamma to her bed room and made her to sit on the cot.

"I want to tell you something very seriously "Jainamma said.

"Why this introduction. Why don't you come straight to the point" Elamma asked?

"Elamma please listen to me. The pre-marital romance and sex amusements may not be that unusual for city girls. For them, that may not be a big issue... But for us it is not like that.... We were brought up in an aristocratic and orthodox Christian family.... We are supposed to maintain certain level of morale and ethics... These acts are considered as sins. You must stop this. How do you know that the boy will keep up his promise and marry you? "How do you know; he won't deceive you? If you continue to live the way you are living now, surely you will regret it one day. You will be cheated Elamma." Jainamma was pleading.

Elamma's face darkened. A hardness reflected in her eyes. She said in an arrogant tone.

"You stop interfering in my affairs. I know how to look after my affairs."

Her voice was sharp and very hostile. Jainamma had never seen such a rude and hostile expression in her sister's face before. Shocked, went sheaway from her room.

Though Elamma had one month leave, she curtailed fifteen days and went back. She was cheerful and active as usual. She did not express any discontent to Jainamma. She acted as if, she had forgotten what Jainmama had discussed the previous night.

"Hey Enasu, will you come on leave in first week of December, to attend our parish feast." Raphel asked

"I don't think I will be able to come. I have already availed my full annual leave. We will come by next December. What is the feast for? ...Pappa."

"December eighth is the day of commemoration of the immaculate conception of saint Mary, mother of Jesus. The church and the local authorities jointly celebrate the festival. It will be a big show with lot of illuminations, decorations and fireworks etc."

"Let me try pappa. But I don't know about the situation there then" He said thoughtfully.

Raphel, Enasu and Jainamma went to the railway station to see Elamma off.

When she left, the house fell silent.

Enasu's leave was also over. There was a crowd at the airport to see them off.

There were five jeeps full of people from Kottackal to bid farewell. The entire relatives of Vazhakkala family also came.

Enasu had a connecting flight from Delhi to Ambala. when they landed, it was four o'clock in the evening. Punjab was burning in the summer heat. It was a bitter experience for Jainamma. She felt as if, she was standing near a furnace. She was tired and helpless.

Flight lieutenant Rajasekharan was waiting to receive them at Ambala airport.

# 7.Cockroach mock

Flight lieutenant Rajasekharan was Enasu's best friend. They were not just best friends but more than that. To put it more correctly, they were two bodies but one soul. They didn't want to keep any secrets between them. However, they had so many secrets to hide. Their lives were being full of secrets.

They were friends from their college days. Both of them studied in 'Maharaja's college, Ernakulam, Cochin. Both graduated in the same subject, physics. Both of them were the main players in the college football team.... Rajasekharan was always the team captain. Enasu had the willingness to give prime position to Rajasekharan. This reciprocal 'give and take' attitude was reflected amongst them throughout their life.

Both were born in 1940. Joined together in Air force in 1960, through campus selection. Both became pilots. Initially they did training on transport and planes later became jet fighter pilots. Both were known as air warriors of 'Hunter' jet fighter aircraft.

Enasu's house was in Vazhakala, in the outskirts of Cochin city. He went to college on his bicycle. Motor bike was not so common at that time.

Rajasekharan's house was in 'Pallikkara' about twenty kilometers away from the college. He used to go to college by bus.

Rajasekharan lost his father when he was studying in tenth standard. Enasu lost his mother when he was only six months of age.

The entire Ernakulam district was developing except for Pallikkara. Pallikkara still remained in its primitive stage, as a remote agricultural village with rubber plantations and paddy fields.

Rajasekharan was born and brought up in an ancestral Hindu family named "Anchumana". Anchumana was a very big house with four facades.

It belonged to four siblings and each facade was for each of them.

Tahasildar Parameswaran Nair, the father of Rajasekharan was the head of the family.

During those days, Thahasildar was the executive magistrate of the region. A powerful man, but his brothers on the contrary were more like thugs of Pallikkara.

Anchumana Parameswaran Nair had very high reputation in the native. He was known as a man of justice and strict adherent of righteousness.

After the partition of wealth among the siblings, Parameswaran Nair was left with four acres of land and the ancient house, Anchumana. It was a high value asset. In those days, as per the Hindu tradition and custom, alliances were made among cousins. Children of siblings married each other. They were called "Murapennu and Murachekkan", meaning predetermined legal bride and groom. Such customs are not being followed now.

Rajasekharan's "Murapennu", (his father's sister's daughter) was Rukmini. Rajasekharan and Rukmini were of the same age. They grew up together and loved each other right from their childhood. The love grew deeper as they reached adolescence.

The great Thahasildar Parameswaran Nair expired when his son Rajasekharan was studying in tenth grade. In his deathbed, a lady named Radha from Paraur reached Anchumana, with her three children, to meet the ailing Parameswaran Nair. She claimed to be Parameswaran Nair's wife. When Parameswaran Nair was working as a village officer in Parur, he was staying in Radha's house as a paying guest. Radha was a spinster at that time. Later they got married in a nearby temple when Radha became pregnant.

The unexpected visit of Radha shocked Anchumana house. There was a big hue and cry. If Parameswaran Nair had not accepted her claim publicly, the lady and her three children would have been killed by the arrogant thug brothers of Parameswaran Nair. But his acceptance turned out to become a big threat in Rajasekharan's life on a later stage.

Flight Lieutenant Rajasekharan was waiting for Enasu and Jainamma, the newly married couple, at the arrival terminal of Ambala civil airport.

Enasu had seen him from far. He was in his Air force uniform. Rajasekharan was standing at the checkout gate talking to an airport officer. A sub inspector of police saluted him and allowed him through the gate.

"Look Jainamma, that man with uniform and with big mustache, is my friend Rajasekharan." Enasu pointed his finger at him.

Jainamma was taken aback by the physical appearance of Rajasekharan. The figure and appearance of Enasu's best friend she had in mind was that of a clean shaved, fair and handsome man like her husband. But what she had seen in reality was entirely different. The man looked like an executioner or a butcher with heavily built body and a handlebar like mustache and dark complexion. Anyone, who sees him is likely to be taken aback, at the sight of that tough looking rough face with chicken pox scars, here and there.

"Oh! is that ruffian your best friend? The very look of him itself is frightening me." Jainamma expressed her dislike. Enasu laughed aloud.

"Jainamma, he looks rough and tough. But he is an innocent soul. Very loving and gentle."

"Is it so.? I doubt that"

"You will realize it, when you associate with him. You will never find such a loving personality anywhere in the world. I will show you now. "He said.

Rajasekharan had seen his friend and his bride coming down by escalators from the arrival parlour. He walked very fast towards them, with a broad smile on his face. When he reached in front of them, Enasu pointed his hand towards the floor and shouted. "Hey look.... cockroach.... cockroach!!!"

Rajasekharan was shocked and he jumped a step back. He looked at the floor with frightened eyes.

Enasu laughed aloud.

When Rajasekharan realized that Enasu was mocking at him, his face became redden in disgrace of his folly.

"Oh...Enasu, I have told you a thousand times, not to mock me with that dirty creature." He said grudgingly.

Enasu laughed again, that made Jainamma also laugh and Rajasekharan joined in.

Jainamma was astonished on noticing, the softness of his voice which was not suitable for a hefty man like him. She was expecting a rough, deep voice. The way he laughed, and his expressions were boyish, which was not at all suitable for a gigantic man with handlebar like mustache.

"Rajasekharan is not afraid of anything on earth other than cockroach. Not even poisonous snakes. When we were in Jorhat, he caught hold of a huge cobra by its neck with his bare hands. But he is very much afraid of the silly insect cockroach." Enasu laughed again.

What he said was not an exaggeration. It was true. It was in 1964. A big cobra happened to get into the kitchen of jorhat Air force mess. It was in the firewood stack adjacent to the kitchen. While the fire wood log was being removed from the stack by a cook, the snake raised its hood and hissed ferociously. The cook cried aloud and ran. All other kitchen staff also got frightened and made a big hue and cry.

Someone ran to the guard room to collect a rifle to shoot it down. Before the arrival of the rifle, Rajasekharan approached the snake from behind with very soft steps. At lightning speed, he caught hold of its neck and lifted it. The snake coiled on his arm with wild wriggles. When everybody stood still, he coolly unwound the snake from his arm and with the help of a cook he put it in a jute bag and tied tightly.

It was a big news in the camp. Rajasekharan was praised for his courage, a hero. Enasu introduced Jainamma to Rajasekharan.

"I am not afraid of cockroach. But I hate that dirty creature. I know it is a psychological impact of a boy hood incident. But I can't help, to overcome the shock." Rajasekharan said to Jainamma.

Enasu had heard of that incident several times. For the sake of Jainamma Rajasekharan narrated the incident while they were walking towards the "parking - lot" where he had parked his car. That incident happened when he was a boy. He was having his meal in the dining room of the tile-roofed house, Anchumana. He was mixing the rice with 'sambar' by his hand, talking to his mother. A cockroach happened to fall in his plate, unnoticed. Unknowingly, he fed himself a scoop of rice with the insect in it. Before chewing it, he felt a thread type thing was protruding out of his mouth. It was its antenna. Without knowing what it was he pulled it out. To his shock, he saw the dirty creature right in front of him in his plate, a cockroach!!!!

He cried out with fright. He vomited out into his plate. Simultaneously, he defecated on his half trousers and fell unconscious. He was rushed to the hospital. Where he was treated for a week. He had very high fever.

"I know it is very silly of me, especially at the age of thirty, to have that much of aversion towards that silly creature. But can't help it. I can't bare the site of that dirty thing."

Rajasekharan laughed like an innocent child. Jainamma was moved by his frankness.

They reached the 'Living out enclave' of Ambala Air Force camp in Rajasekharan's car. Throughout the drive, he was talking continuously, and laughing joyously. Jainamma remembered what Enasu had told her about his friend. 'He looks very rough and tough but he is an innocent soul.'

A well furnished two bed room family quarters was allotted to Enasu. It was a comfortable house with all modern amenities.

Jainamma checked all the rooms and facilities and was satisfied. Rajasekharan had already procured almost all the provisions and grocery items and had stored them in the kitchen. Sufficient food stuff also was stored in the refrigerator.

How caring he is! She was astonished and very much impressed.

"Hey Jainamma please, give us a cup of tea. You may light the gas stove and inaugurate the kitchen. By the way, you know how to cook right?" Rajasekharan asked.

"She is a great cook." Enasu answered. "Her chicken curry prepared in coconut milk is awesome; My father praised her a lot for that dish."

"Oh...that is wonderful. One day I will try your chicken curry."

"You are welcome. Please come with Rukmini. We will have dinner here." Jainamma had extended the invitation very pleasingly.

"To have a dinner with Rukmini, we may have to go to Pallikara." Rajasekharan said.

"Why, is she not in your quarters, where is your quarters? I am very eager to meet Rukmini."

"I have no family quarters here. I am staying in bachelors' billet in the mess."

"Why?" Jainamma asked in astonishment "Have you not brought Rukmini here?"

"No." Then Rajasekharan told his story.

Rukmini was of his age' and was a school teacher at Pallikkara. She was his aunt's daughter. Her mother and his father are cousins. As per Hindu tradition and custom, she was his 'Murapennu'. That means she was his customary proposed bride.

She was her parents' only child. Her parents died in 1948 in a boat accident. Rukmini was only eight years old then. She was brought to Anchumana house by his father. Rukmini was looked after by his mother. Rajasekharan and Rukmini had grown up together in Anchumana. During adolescence age they became lovers. No one was there to control their adolescent gestures and infatuations. Later Rajasekharan's mother also became sick and was confined to bed. Rukmini was looking after her.

"Still my ailing mother is being looked after by Rukmini. We were living like a husband and wife for the past ten years. As long as my mother is in her sick bed, I am not in a position to bring her here. We don't have anyone to take care of my mother." Rajasekharan sighed. "I can't pray for the death of my mother.

Suddenly his eyes were moist, his face reddened. It was evident that he was suppressing his feelings inside his heart.

Rajasekharan got up and said, "I have ordered dinner for you in our mess. It will be delivered here by seven thirty. .'Pulavu', chicken curry and vegetables are in the menu for today. Have your dinner and take rest. Tomorrow onwards you may prepare your own food".

Rajasekharan bid farewell and left.

Enasu and Jainamma started their family life in that Air force quarters in April 1971.

## 8. Cloud of war

Enasu had a memorable honeymoon period and a wonderful family life in Ambala Air Force camp. The couple enjoyed their life to the fullest. Jainamma was liked by everybody in the camp. She was the most beautiful house wife in the camp. Her presence was encouraged and welcomed in parties and social gatherings. When Jainamma was pregnant with her very first child, Enasu's friends and acquaintances were very caring and considerate towards her and her health.

One day Jainamma requested her maid to get an unripe mango to quench her pregnancy craving. There was no unripe mango available at that time in the vegetable shops nearby. Somehow, Enasu's friends came to know about her desire for the raw mangoes. That night, ten big baskets full of unripe mangoes were brought to their quarters by his colleges. They had plucked the mangoes from trees and brought it from a far away village. Later, Enasu had to give away all those mangoes to the mess to make pickle.

Enasu was heading for a period of hardship and misfortune. He had to face a series of tragedies, one after another. He was tortured mentally and physically by fate.

It all started when India-Pakistan border dispute became worse. General Yahyakhan, the military ruler of Pakistan was taking revenge on India, for supporting Bangladesh to get them liberated from the iron first of the military dictator. Pakistan soldiers started to violate the border rules deliberately, to create problems. In Punjab sector a battalion of Pakistani soldiers crossed the Indian border and looted a few villages. They reaped paddy fields and took away the yields to Pakistan. A few Pakistani soldiers were killed in the clash between Pakistan and India, which made Pakistan ruler furious. The

Pakistan General through the radio threatened to bombard Delhi, if India attacked Pakistan. It was the most defiant statement of the Pak- General. As far as India was concerned, if Pakistan ever draged India into a war, it would be a catastrophe for Pakistan as it would never be able to defend itself and win over India.

America openly supported Pakistan and it was very unexpected. They moved their sixth fleet into Indian Ocean to support the Pak force. As a challenge to USA, Russia supported India and they had positioned their fifth fleet in the Bay of Bengal. A world war was predicted by some papers and political viewers.

The whole world was watching with curiosity, how the situation would turn out to be. Indira Gandhi, the Prime Minister of India boldly declared that no external support was needed, and India was capable of handling the situation alone. If Pakistan ever had the guts to attack India, without any hesitation, India would reciprocate and defend itself and make its stand clear. It was roar of a she lion.

Indira Gandhi addressed the nation over radio and asked everyone to be prepared for a war. India's sovereignty and integrity had been challenged. "National emergency" was declared. All the military campuses were given alert orders. Army started to move towards the border. Fighter aircrafts were positioned in various Air bases in the border sector. The Prime Minister had personally visited all Air Force camps to motivate airmen and fighter pilots.

When the Prime Minister visited Ambala Air Base, she had dinner with fighter pilots in a separate hall in officers' mess. It was a great motivation and honour for the pilots.

While everyone was sitting and having their first course soup, the Prime Minister called Enasu by his name, to the surprise of everyone. Enasu got up from his seat, walked swifty with soup spoon in his hand and stood in attention in front of the Prime Minister.

"Sit Down, Flight Lieutenant Enasu. You may please have dinner with me." The Prime Minister invited.

Everyone was dumbstruck. It was a great honour for Enasu. A plate was placed in front of him and food was served. While having food, the Prime Minister talked to him in a very casual, manner.

"You are a family man aren't you?"

"Yes mam" Enasu answered politely.

"Your commanding officer was telling me that your wife is carrying now."

"Yes mam. It is the seventh month of pregnancy"

"Good. Congratulations! By the way, where are you planning to have her delivery?

That was an unexpected question.

"In our military hospital Madam".

"Why don't you send her home?"

The suggestion surprised Enasu. The commanding officer, who was seated beside her, was looking at his plate and was pretending to be busy eating, though he was just fiddling with his spoon and fork.

"Mam, both of us do not have mothers, our fathers are aged and we have no siblings at home to help. We don't want to give trouble to our fathers. Moreover our gynecologist Dr. Sandra is very efficient and one of the best. Besides that, the facilities provided in our military hospital is better than any hospitals in kerala." Enasu explained.

"What are you talking Enasu? We have a wonderful Naval hospital at Cochin. Sanjeevini Hospital is one of the best military hospitals in

Kerala. Why can't you plan her delivery over there? I will personally call the Commanding Officer of Cochin Naval Base and ask him to make necessary arrangements in this regard. They will take care of your wife better than your relatives."

"But Ma'am"

Enasu wanted to tell something. The prime Minister did not allow him to talk further.

In a serious tone she said, "Listen Enasu, we are going in for a war. Don't disclose information about this matter to anyone till we declare it officially. Not even to your close friends or wife. We are anticipating the war to be very severe. Pakistan is very likely to attack our Air Base as well. If so, things would be very serious and intense. I don't want your wife to panic or get upset, when you are in the war front. And one more thing, you are one of the selected fighter pilots of our "task force" she said.

The prime minister's casual talk turned out to be highly official and very authoritative order. Enasu felt a sudden chill down his spine and had a dreadful feeling that something serious was about to happen.

Enasu clearly understood what the authoritative Prime Minister meant. She had clear, well framed and calculated plans about the forthcoming war. The war would be very fierce. His life would be at stake, being a warrior of the Task Force. Once assigned for bombing or strafing there won't be any surety of return.

For the first time in his life, Enasu thought about his death and got frightened as he did not want to die. He had someone to wait for him. Jainamma his loving wife and their Soon-to-be-born, child, whom Enasu was longing to meet.

Enasu became upset and worried.

The very next day, Enasu was ordered to take Jainamma home. They were flown by helicopter piloted by Rajasekharan from Ambala to Delhi airport, and from there by Indian Airlines flight to Cochin.

He was advised to return from Cochin by the next available train.

An Ambulance from Cochin Naval base was waiting for them at Cochin Airport. They were given a VIP reception at airport which astonished Enasu.

Arrival of pregnant Jainamma brought joy and happiness in Kottakal family at Kothamangalam. Elamma also was present there when they arrived home. She came two days back, for her forty-five days leave which was saved from her annual leave, so that she could attend the church feast and Christmas.

On hearing the news, Vazhakala Devassy, the father of Enasu reached Kottakal to meet his son and the pregnant daughter- in-law and his son.

"You should have stepped into our house at kakkanadukara, and visited your aged father. It was only a five kilometers deviation."

Devassy complained but with a lot of love and affection in his words.

"Oh... Appa, it was not deliberate. From airport we were travelling in an ambulance till here", Enasu Said.

"Ambulance? Oh...my God. Is she sick? Is there any problem?". The loving father got worried.

"Oh...No..Jainamma is a VIP now. She is our Prime Minister's guest now."

"Prime Minister...? Indira Gandhi?" All were bewildered.

Rajasekharan's trunk call was received by Raphel in the morning, that Enasu and Jainamma would reach there by noon. Immediately Devassy telephoned Kakkanadukara and informed Devassy. Overjoyed he invited all his friends and relatives to welcome his pregnant daughter. There was a big crowd at Kottakkal house when they arrived.

Enasu explained in front of everyone, how the Prime Minister happened to intervene in Jainamma's case.

"When her delivery is due, just call this number. The ambulance with doctor and nurse will come here and take Jainamma to Cochin Naval base hospital." Enasu said proudly, and gave Raphel a card.

That night there was a big feast at Kottakkal house. But the very next day the Kottakkal house plunged into great disappointment, as Elamma received a telegram from her hospital. Her leave was cancelled and was ordered to report for duty. Since it was an order, Elamma had to comply and there was no other go. Though everyone knew about the military rules regarding leave no one expected that, it was applicable for nurses too. However, Raphel was relieved that his daughter Elamma did not have to travel alone since Enasu was there to accompany her up to Delhi. He considered, it as God's blessing.

But he never knew, that it would turn out to be a curse.

It was very difficult to get reserved seats in the train at short notice. Since all the military personnel were being called back for duty, there was heavy rush in the train and Enasu somehow managed to get a coupe with two births, by paying heavy bribe to the booking officer.

The travel time to Delhi was forty-eight hours, Two nights and one and a half days.

The first two hours of journey was very embarrassing for both Enasu and Elamma, since they were alone in the coupe. Slowly the discomforts had melted away and an intimacy developed between them.

Elamma started talking freely. She giggled, cracked jokes, and laughed aloud. Naughtiness reflected in all her actions and behavior and Enasu enjoyed her company.

"Jainamma is so lucky to get a wonderful husband like you." Elamma said with envy and a slight disappointment in her voice.

"Hey...why did you say that? The marriage proposal was for you, and you rejected me!" Enasu said smiling.

Elamma's face fell "oh...at that time I was in love with that stupid fellow Captain Roy."

"Both of you were in deep love and planned to get married, that was what you told me then. Remember?"

Her face flushed red and eyes moistened. "It was a mistake. A grave mistake. I was a fool...to trust him blindly."

Tears trickled down her cheeks. Enasu felt pity for her.

"He wanted my body alone and not my love, He never loved me. He is a bloody cheat...cheat!!!"

She started to sob and all of a sudden, she burst out crying aloud. Enasu was taken aback. He didn't know how to console and calm her down.

"Don't cry Elamma. Please don't cry. Past is past, try and forget about it. That is the only wise thing you can do now. Crying about your past is a foolish thing. ..." He wanted to say something further, but he was short of words. She continued crying hysterically.

In order to console her, he caressed her head very mildly with sympathy and affection. Suddenly, Elamma leaned on to his chest and clinched him with both her hands as if he was the only refuge for her and cried. Her body was pressed against him very tightly.

Enasu was stunt and bewildered. The warmth of her body and the fragrance from her hair sent a hot wave through his veins. He wanted to get away from her. He tried to move away from her. But her grip was too strong to release and the intensity of her weeping increased. Unconsciously his hands circled her and under the influence of hormonal rush, he could not control himself and fell into a fantasy. He became fully aroused.

She panted in his ear" Have me...Have me...." and fell on the sleeper birth along with him.

On the third day, the train reached Delhi. All the three days they lost sight of everything around and fell into the thrill of infatuation and fantasy. Their sense of morale and virtue were compromised and they absolutely disregarded ethics and virtues.

When they arrived at Delhi, Elamma was reluctant to part. She wanted to stay in a hotel for a day with Enasu, and she insisted that he stayed back with her, but Enasu refused. He came back to his sense, and realised the seriousness of his actions. He had committed a sin, he disregarded all virtues. He also knew, he was heading for deep trouble. Enasu wanted to come out of it but Elamma wanted to stick on with him.

She had affirmed that she would visit Ambala whenever she got a chance.

"Don't be a stupid. If Jainamma happened to know about this, she would kill us both." He said, in a frightened voice. He was suffering a pang of conscience.

"Oh.... that I will take care. She will never know. I know how to manage her. She is innocent, like an infant." She said.

Elamma's 'don't care' attitude frightened Enasu. He realized that he was under the grip of a venomous octopus, who wouldn't let go off him that easily.

A devilish thought of eliminating her forever without leaving any evidence came in his mind.

## 9. The war

It was dark when Enasu reached Ambala Air Force Camp. His heart was also in darkness with self-hatred and guilty conscience. He even thought of committing suicide. The thought of future consequences had frightened him.

The entire North West region of India was in pitch darkness as, blackout was declared. A threat of war was prevailing everywhere. People were in panic. All schools and colleges in that area were closed.

Intrusions of Pakistani troops into Indian Territory were reported throughout the border. The Indian Army had encountered them in many places. So many people were killed. Many Indian soldiers were martyred. There was a general uneasiness prevailing everywhere, and everyone anticipated a war. A fierce war!

As anticipated, the dreadful war began. On 3rd December night Pakistan bombarded Indian Territory. They dropped a number of bombs, in towns and villages near the border. A few army camps were also attacked. Indian Air Force was very vigilant and alert. Radar eyes were wide open. Fifteen Indian aircrafts took off from three different airbases simultaneously for the encounter. There was a fierce "dog fight" in midair between Pakistani F104 jets and Indian "Hunter" supersonic jets. Gnat aircrafts were flying high above as "cap" to guide the fighting Hunter jets.

India lost five aircraft's in that mission and Pakistan lost seven planes.

"I am not worried about the loss of aircrafts. But I am deadly worried and upset about the loss of the lives of our air warriors."

The Prime Minister Indira Gandhi's voice message echoed in the sector operation centre (SOC).

There were a series of air attacks and India, efficiently blocked all of them. There were ten to twelve 'sorties' by squadrons every day. The casualties were very high. Thirty-two aircrafts were shot down by Pakistani, Radar guided high range guns. Indian war tacticians started worrying. Counter argument that the enemy had lost more numbers of aircraft did not satisfy the Prime Minister.

Sargodha air force station was the nerve centre of Pakistani forces. The war was controlled from Sargodha. They had a big runway and a very huge underground hangar in which hundreds of aircrafts could be parked. They were operating four squadrons from Sargodha. Their American made radar had a coverage of four hundred kilometers. Large numbers of radar controlled anti-aircraft guns were fitted around Sargodha. It was impossible to approach Sargodha by air or by land. Sargodha became a nightmare to Indian war tacticians.

India formed an Air Task Force (ATF), of brave brilliant air warriors, including Enasu and Rajasekharan. Such an Air Task Force was formed during second world war, but none of the ATF members survived. The Air Task Force was known as "suicide squad". Once a task is given to ATF none will return without its accomplishment, that was the role and rule of the ATF

That night, Prime Minister along with Air Chief Marshal, PC Lal landed at Ambala Air Base in an "llyushin" VIP aircraft. Six ATF pilots were called at Air Traffic Control(ATC) briefing room. The Prime Minister talked to them very confidentially.

"Gentlemen, the mission assigned to you is a tough task. A life-threatening task. Sargodha will be your target. To intrude into Sargodha air space is a nearly impossible task that I am aware of, but we have to take a chance, without which we cannot win this war. If we lose, we will not be able to raise our head in front of the world. It is a matter of our pride and prestige. Even if we get one percent chance to strike them down, don't hesitate. Hit hard and smash them forever. I am confident that you are capable of achieving your goal. I am proud of you. If you succeed, the nation will praise you and you will be ever remembered. It doesn't matter if you win or lose. An attempt itself is a great service to the nation. We are applying a very special tactics here. The formation no.1 will make advance attack. They will chase you. At that time, formation no.2 will intrude. "If there is no chance to intrude you may abort the mission and return. But try. Is it clear?" she asked.

"Yes mam" the ATF warriors replied boldly.

" Are you ready, gentlemen?". The Prime Minister asked again by looking at their faces.

"Yes, mam." The replies were very brave and bold.

They could see their Prime Minister's eyes were moistened. They were overwhelmed. Their hearts were filled with patriotism. They raised their strong fists in the air and said aloud.

"Jai Hind!!!!" (Hail India)

The Prime Minister did not respond. She was not in a position to open her mouth to say anything. Her throat was choked with an upsurging sob.

The time was 12.30 in the midnight. The entire North West India was under the cover of pitch darkness due to black out. The sky was cloudy. The dim crescent moon was peeping through the cloud. No stars were seen.

Six 'Hunter' fighter aircrafts loaded with missile warheads and 20 mm guns lined up in the runway in two formations of three aircrafts each. Two high powered bombs were fitted under the fuselage of each aircraft. With thundering roars, the aircrafts took off, one after the other. They made an arrow formation, in mid-air and headed towards 'Sargodha' at an altitude of fifty thousand feet which was above surveillance Radar Coverage.

Within minutes they reached above the target. Though 'Sargodha' was under the cover of thick blanket of darkness, the flight radar indicator had clearly shown the exact locations of each vital points. After three orbits they descended to a lower level.

The response was quick. They were detected by the Pakistan Radar. Air sirens were blasted all over 'Sargodha'. The entire camp had shuddered and had woken up with wilderness. Hundreds of Anti Aircraft guns fired simultaneously. Their bullets were seen flying like fire balls all over the sky and formed protective umbrella over 'Sargodha'. The pilots could see the ground in the red light of fired bullets. Hundreds of aircrafts were parked in the tarmac in two rows. They did see the wide opening of the underground hangar, where bombers were parked. But there was no chance to pierce through the bullet arrows.

Rajasekharan, the formation commander was afraid. He realized that, the mission would not be accomplished. He was about to order his subordinate fighters to abort the attempt and return to base. But suddenly he heard a wild roar of Enasu through the Radio phone.

"Rajan, Gupta .... Dive...Dive...Dive...." The roar was loud and ear blasting. Enasu made a daring Zig-Zag dive towards the target below through the upsurging bullet arrows, at lightning speed, crossing the sound barrier, resulting a high pitched thunder sound. Gupta followed him like a whirlwind.

Rajasekharan could not follow him. He was frightened to death when he saw thousands of fire balls in front of him, like fireworks. He did not have the courage to advance. He did not want to get himself killed. He had fled from the battle field, others followed him.

That was a fierce and dreadful assault Enasu had performed. He strafed continuously with 18mm guns fitted under both the wings of aircraft at the rows of fighter jets parked in the tarmac. There were hundreds of them. All of them were loaded with warheads. There were explosions and wildfire. He could fire one missile through the hangar door where bombers were parked. One missile had smashed the huge radar unit. He had seen the gigantic radar areal collapse. He dropped both the bombs fitted under the fuselage of aircraft exactly at the centre of the runway. He was sure, that it will take months for the enemy to make the runway useable again. He flew high to flee. All finished within thirty seconds. If he could fly two more minutes, he would have crossed the border and escaped. Before he could escape, his plane was hit by a ground to air missile. The target was precise and point blank. It hit at the nozzle of his aircraft. He managed to pull the bailout trigger in time just before the aircraft exploded in midair. He was thrown out of the aircraft along with his seat. The seat detached from him and the parachute opened. From the exploded aircraft, a metallic object stuck on his knee and pierced through the knee cap. He felt a sudden numbness at his knee and spread through the vein up to his brain. His eyesight blurred and he became unconscious in midair hanging on the parachute.

When he opened his eyes he realized he had fallen down in the midst of wild thorny plants. His parachute was lying beside him. He had seen the barbed wire fence of India - Pak border and an Indian bunker with national flag flying high. He could see Indian soldiers standing outside the bunker with their rifles in their hands. Luckily, he was in safer area where Pakistan bunkers were not in vicinity. He wanted to shout for help. No voice came out of his throat. He could not move his left leg. It felt very heavy like a cement bag kept on his leg. This leg was numb and the entire body was in pain.

With great struggle he crawled out of the thicket and shouted. A soldier noticed him. He shouted something and others came out of the bunker. Within minutes they cut the fences with cutter and rescued him from the Pakistan territory. At that time Enasu was unconscious.

## 10. Miraculous escape

Enasu was very lucky to have landed near an Indian outpost bunker closer to the border fence though in Pakistan land.

In between the two countries, there were two lines of barbed fences in the border. One at the boundary of the Pakistan. And other at Indian boundary with ten-meter gap in between the two boundaries. The ten meters wide vacant area in between the two security fencies was known as 'No man's land'. Enasu had landed inside the Pakistan's territory. Indian Army men had to cut both the fences to rescue Enasu. There were no Pakistani soldiers in the vicinity and the location was thirty kilometers north side of Amritsar Air Force Camp. Enasu was taken to the camp hospital by jeep. He was unconscious and looked dead when he reached hospital. He had lost a lot of blood. His left knee was severely crushed and looked like a beetroot, smashed by a hammer. Many portions of the knee cap were missing. He had very high temperature and the leg was cold. He was affected with 'fat embolism'.

Fat getting into blood stream is fat embolism' and it is fatal. It could cause death or coma, if not attended immediately.

Enasu was transferred to Ludhiana military hospital by helicopter immediately. He was in ICU for thirty-five days to get cured from fat embolism and pneumonia. He had to undergo a major surgery on his left leg. The Prime Minister of India had visited Ludhiana military hospital twice to meet Enasu. Both the times he was under sedation.

Within two days of Sargodha's fall the war ended. Sargodha was the nerve centre of Pakistan's war operations. Enasu could smash that nerve. There was no other go for General Yahia Khan than to raise the white flag of peace and surrender. India could raise the victory flag high with pride.

"The nation will be ever indebted to the brave warriors of Indian air force who had assaulted Sargodha to lead India to Victory." The Prime

Minister made a special mention of the task in her speech to the nation. But she never mentioned, about the formation of suicide squad and the names of the air warriors who were involved. It was kept as a military secret.

Flight lieutenant Gupta, one of the STF pilots who had sacrificed his life for the nation in Sargodha was awarded with VSM "posthumously."

Enasu was awarded with 'AVSM', the higher gallantry award for bravery. The news flashed in the radio and newspapers. Malayalam papers published the news in front page with a photo of Enasu in uniform.

The entire natives of Kerala were thrilled to have a war hero from their land. The family members of Vazhakala at Kakkanadukara and Kottakkal at Kothamangalam felt proud. Jainamma's eyes were moistened due to overjoy. But no one knew about the daring task Enasu had performed.

Rajasekharan was not aware that Enasu was alive when the war ended. He had seen the number of Enasu's hunter aircraft in the 'lost list' published in SRO, Station routine orders. Its number was just below the number of Gupta's ill-fated plane. He presumed that Enasu also had become a martyr and he wept.

Rajasekharan was transferred to Delhi Air force camp with a promotion. He resumed his new assignment as Squadron Commander.

There was an urgent telegram for Rajasekharan from Rukmini. It read "Mother expired. Start immediately".

Rajasekharan was granted with sixty days' immediate annual leave. He could reach Pallikara within six hours on receipt of the telegram, which astonished everybody. One hour waiting at Delhi airport and four hours flying to Cochin by Indian Airlines flight. One hour by taxi to Pallikara from Cochin airport. He could perform the pre-cremation rites and rituals for his mother.

On the sixth day of cremation Rajasekharan received a trunk call from his commanding officer. He had called Rajasekharan to convey his condolences.

"I have good news for you, Rajasekharan." The commanding officer Air commodore Marva said.

"What is it sir? "Rajasekharan asked.

"Your friend, Enasu had a miraculous escape. He could bail out from the aircraft before it exploded. He was rescued by army, and was admitted in Ludhiana military hospital."

It was a great news! He was overwhelmed with joy. "How is he sir? any serious injury?" He asked

"Details are not known; I am afraid he may lose his leg. His knee was scattered in explosion."

Rajasekharan was shocked. He wanted to cry aloud. He could not imagine his friend in crutches without a leg. He wanted to reach his friend at the earliest.

The "Sanjayanam", a ceremony collecting of bones of cremated person from the pyre and immersing in the river is a religious rite, was arranged for the next day. Such rituals are very important for Hindus, which was meant to get salvation of the soul of the dead.

Rajasekharan had performed the 'Sanjayanam' and conducted the "Srath" (serving food to who attend the sanjayanam). That was also a part of the rites.

He locked the house and gate of 'Anchumana' and handed over the keys to his uncle, to take care of the property and house, and left Pallikkara with

Rukmini. He was in hurry to reach Ludhiana hospital to meet Enasu. He was very much embarrassed to face his friend with an amputated leg.

He took over the 'family quarters' assigned to him in west block New Delhi and started his "living out" with Rukmini.

He drove himself in his car to Ludhiana military hospital to meet Enasu. He was still in ICU. To his relief, it was revealed to him that his leg would not be amputated. The Prime Minister had arranged medical experts from Germany to treat Enasu. Specially developed prosthesis, an artificial knee, would be imported to be placed on his leg.

"He will walk for sure, after the replacement of knee. I am sure he will play football with his artificial knee." The German doctor assured Rajasekharan. However, the medical board of hospital had decided to 'Board Out' Enasu from service, as he was a handicap and would be unfit for flying. Their recommendation was forwarded to the ministry for approval. The case was brought to the notice of the Prime Minister, and she called for the file. The air marshal also was called. She made him to issue a confidential order as under.

**The case of war victim Flt.Lt. Enasu**

1. Flt.Lt. Enasu who is admitted in Ludhiana military hospital is promoted to the rank of wing commander bypassing the immediate rank of Squadron leader. It is a double promotion rewarded for the excellent service rendered by him in 1971 war, rewarded by the President of India the Supreme Commander of Armed force vide the power vested in him as per prevailing rules.
2. He is allowed to continue in active service for ground duties till his superannuation. The recommendations for 'Board out' forwarded by the medical council is rejected and returned.

3. He is transferred to Delhi and assigned as Air Traffic controller of Delhi. The above posting is nontransferable and permanent in nature.

4. He should be allotted with a family quarters immediately on his discharge from hospital.

The special order was first of its kind and very new to Indian Air Force. After replacement of knee with imported prosthesis Enasu could walk, though with the help of a walking stick. He was transferred to Delhi Air force hospital for advanced physiotherapy treatment. The therapy included basketball playing.

Rajasekharan was promoted as Squadron Leader and posted at New Delhi. That made Rajasekharan and Rukmini regular visitors of Enasu in Delhi hospital and they used to spend hours together.

## 11. Old aged home

Fr. Robin Padippura, the parish priest of Kothamangalam village church was a close friend of Kottackkal Raphel, the widower and father of Jainamma and Elamma. The priest used to visit Kottakkal house very often. He was of the same age as Raphel, about fifty-five years, and both were very fond of chess. Raphel was the trustee of the church, and Fr. Robin was the vicar.

When Jainamma, came home with her child after the delivery at Naval Base Hospital, Cochin, the routine chess game had come to an end because Raphel became very busy in playing and cuddling his grandchild, Ancy.

The child was baptized by Fr. Robin and the pet name 'Ancy' was given by him, meaning "beautiful of all". The child was very beautiful and cute. Jainamma wanted to baptize the child after Enasu's arrival but since, it would take months for him to come on leave, they decided to conduct the ceremony in his absence.

"Let the child be christened now and later when Enasu comes, we can arrange the celebrations". Fr. Robin insisted.

Fr. Robin was running an old age home with six inmates, which included his own father. In fact, he started the old age home to look after his father and later admitted some more aged people as inmates.

Fr. Robin had three brothers who were wealthy. Two of them were settled in Canada and the youngest brother stayed at their ancestral house. He was henpecked and his wife Susy a school teacher was very rude to his aged father. One day Fr. Robin made a visit to his father. He felt that his father was very uncomfortable and upset.

"It was a great mistake that I allowed you to go for priesthood. If you were married and had a family, I could have come and lived with you, my son. I am fed up and wondering why God almighty is not having the mercy to take me to his abode and end my suffering in here." The old man lamented, then wept holding his son's hand.

Fr. Robin was deeply moved by what his dear father had said. He confronted regarding this to his sister -in -law Susy which, he soon regretted.

The lady turned angrily to remonstrate with him. She started to accuse the old man and started listing a series of complains about him. He was very untidy and filthy, he urinated in bed, never happy in anything she did and she went on and on....

"Son!! Could you please take me to an old age home or orphanage or any similar institutions? I can't take it any longer, you are a priest, you may know about some place that I can go to and take refuge in." His father sobbed, Fr. Robin also wept.

"Hey Robin!! There are no problems as you think. Father is simply accusing Susy as he is mentally not stable. He is having some mental disorder that's what Susy says" His brother told to pacify Robin.

For the very first time in his life, Robin raised his hand and slapped his younger brother on his cheek. Everyone was shocked. Susy came running towards Robin and wanted to say something, harshly.

"If you open your mouth Lady, I will slap you too."

Robin said in a stern voice. Susy got terrified and she cried aloud.

Robin helped his father to get dressed, collected all his belongings, medicines and bedpan, then called a taxi and left the house with his father without uttering a word to his brother and his wife.

He brought him to the 'priest's house' and made him comfortable in his room. There was a vacant old house, near the church which was the priests, house earlier. When the new house was constructed the old one was abandoned for demolishing. With the help of altar boys and church committee he made that house usable and his father was shifted there. Sexton was asked to look after him with remuneration. When the parishioners came to know that the aged man was their vicar's father, they were happy to take care of him. They fed him, they nursed him and they treated and respected him as their own father.

Fr. Robin came to know, that there was another aged parent in his parish totally ignored by his rich son. He voluntarily brought him and accommodated with his father. The rich son was not a miser. He donated one lakh rupees to Fr. Robin to develop the old age home. Later he found out there were four more ignored aged parents living in misery. He went to their homes and brought them voluntarily, and advised their children, to remit some amount every month towards their expenditure.

An idea of establishing a well facilitated old age home cropped up in Fr. Robin's mind. He started to work on it. He went to Kottakkal house to meet Raphel to discuss the subject.

Raphel was standing at the gate of his house with Ancy, his grandchild, in his arms. The child was very fond of looking at vehicles passing through. Whenever she saw a vehicle coming from far she would shake her legs and body violently to express her thrill, and Raphel enjoyed her actions.

Fr. Robin discussed the subject with Raphel while walking towards the house. They were seated in the drawing room. Jainamma came to the room and picked up the child from her father.

"Hey Jainamma, any news about your sister Elamma?"

Fr. Robin asked.

"I received a letter from her two months back. She wrote that she was with Red cross society"

"Yes...Yes...that's true. There were huge civilian casualties during the war. Red cross people would work jointly with military to rehabilitate the victims of war."

"She wrote, not to send letter to her. If needed, she would call." Jainamma said.

"Yes...Yes...they will be very busy. What about your husband the war hero? Our church is planning to give him a big reception on his arrival. He is our parish's pride."

"He is in Ludhiana, undergoing some special coaching, he told me..."

"Yes...Yes...good...good....God bless you." Convey my regards to him.

When Jainamma left the room with the child, Fr. Robin opened the old age home subject again.

"We must provide a good accommodation for ten to twelve people to begin with. I am planning a luxurious old age home to accommodate rich people. From what I understand, rich people are ready to spend any amount, if someone is willing to take the burden of looking after their parents. I want to take advantage of this attitude of the rich and do as much as I can to serve the old and needy people.

"Why don't you plan to start your old age home in this house?" Raphel asked. "We have fourteen rooms in this house. Though constructed about one hundred and fifty years ago, all the rooms are in perfect condition. Some rooms we don't open at all. This house was constructed by my grandfather. At that time, ours was a joint family. If you take this house, I will construct a small house and shift to there. But, that is possible only after Elamma's marriage".

"It is a nice idea. Any way, we will discuss the subject later". Fr. Robin said.

## 12. Sin bites back

It was a rebirth for Enasu. The doctors treated him never expected that he would survive. The air crash in Pak territory and the mode of assault on Sargodha was kept as a military secret. Assignment of a suicide squad to attack a Nation was against the International Humanitarian Law, as per Geneva Convention. India did not want to get tangled with in any controversy by giving a detailed account of the operation.

It was August 15th, 1972, the last day of Enasu's hospital life. He had stayed in hospital for eight months. It was planned that Rajasekharan would go to hospital by eleven o'clock to take him to the new quarters allotted to him. It was also planned that Enasu would avail his annual leave, and bring Jainamma and child to stay with him in family quarters. Enasu was longing to see the tiny face of his new born child... Ancy.

He was allotted with family quarters No.45 in south block New Delhi, just adjacent to Rajasekharan's quarters No.46 in same building.

Rajasekharan reached hospital very early. Enasu seemed to be very active and energetic. He was limping while walking, otherwise he was perfect. For the last one week he was playing basketball along with other arthroplasty patients as a part of their physiotherapy.: There were thirty such patients in the hospital. All were war victims, out of whom Enasu was the only knee replacement patient.

"Why did you come so early? I did not have my bath yet. I have to have my breakfast also." Enasu said.

"Then hurry up... We have to go quickly." Rajasekharan said, looking irritated.

Enasu looked at him and wondered. "What happened to you? Your face is looking very dull. You were in a happy mood yesterday. Suddenly what happened overnight"?

Rajasekharan's face was swollen as if he was suppressing some agony in him. His eyes werelooked very upset. This expression in Rajasekharan was strange to Enasu.

"Hey...what happened to you Raja? Did you take your drink early in the morning? It is very unusual of you.... why?"

Rajasekharan looked at his friend. There was lot of haterdedness in his eyes; that worried Enasu.

"Hey tell me man... What's wrong" .... Enasu became furious.

"I never knew you are such a stupid and untrustworthy man. "... Rajasekharan abused him in harsh voice.

Enasu was shocked. His friend never talked to him in that manner, ever before.

"What the hell are you talking? .... I don't understand. What's wrong?... What have I done to you?" .... Enasu pleaded.

He felt hurt.... His eyes became moistened.

"I never knew you were double-faced and that you tried to hide your devilish side from me for all these years"

"Why are you being so cruel to this handicapped man, Raja tell me frankly how I hurt you man?"

"You have never hurt me...... You can't, *you* will never, I know that, but you hurt that poor girl Elamma, your wife's sister". Rajasekharan growled with grief and anger.

"Elamma"! Enasu's eyes widened in wonder and he was taken aback.

"Yes, Elamma. She is in your quarters... waiting for you".

Enasu thought that, she might have come to stay with him to quench her hunger for lust. He remembered what she had told him, when they parted, after the train journey.

"It is only a five-hour journey from here to Ambala. If I get one day off from duty, I can reach there and stay with you one night."

"Oh...Elamma.... That bitch.! What does she want"? Enasu asked irritably.

"Shut up!!!!" Rajasekharan shouted angrily.

"She is pregnant and in advanced stage of pregnancy. She is very weak, fragile and dead tired. She can't walk or even talk. She had to be hospitalized immediately. That's why I came in a hurry. She said she is bearing your child.... can you deny that?" Rajasekharan asked emotionally.

Enasu felt as if, a thunder stuck him. Suddenly he felt weak and numb. He could not stand further. He sat on his bed in utter desperation. He felt as if the entire world was whirling around him. He looked at his friend helplessly.

Rajasekharan sat on a chair facing him.

"She says that, she is bearing your child in her womb ... Is it true?"

"If she said so, yes it is true."

"How dare you!!" Rajasekharan was furious. But he controlled himself and asked mildy. "How did that happen man? You were always a man of ethics and principle.... What happened???"

Enasu covered his face with his hands and wept like a child. Rajasekharan just sat there looking at him. After a few minutes, he started narrating the whole incident, looking down in despair.

"It was unexpected. Very unfortunate, not deliberate. I did not have any intention even to touch her. But...But...It happened. It was my mistake. I should have controlled myself and be a bit more cautious. I lost my self-control. It was my mistake,"

He wept again, shedding tears uncontrollably.

They checked out from the hospital and drove to quarters silently. Both of them were thinking about ways to come out of the precarious situation. Enasu's mind was frantically searching for ways to erase Elamma from his life forever.

Elamma was lying in a bed in Enasu's quarters. She was the first to step in that house prior to Enasu. The new quarters were allotted in his name, while he was in hospital. It was under the custody of Rajasekharan, and the key was with him.

Elamma looked very sick and tired. Her chubbiness was completely gone and became very thin and skinny. Her belly was abnormally protruded. Her eyes were closed and she was groaning restlessly.

Enasu felt pity on her, yet he didn't want her to disturb him.

"How did she reach here in this condition? How did she find out that, this is my quarters?" Enasu asked.

"Early morning, I got a call from the guard room. The sergeant on duty told me that a pregnant lady said to be your wife came in a taxi and asked for you. Since, the sergeant knew that you are in hospital he called me. I went there and found Elamma sitting on a chair tired and desperate. When I introduced myself to her, she revealed everything...everything...Poor girl."

There was lot of sympathy in his voice.

"After all you are a nurse... You should have done something to terminate it at the beginning itself, that's what sensible people do." Enasu accused her.

Nobody was sure whether she heard or not. She continued to groan and cry.

"She tried" Rukmini raised her voice as she was defending Elamma and ridiculed Enasu.

"We had a little conversation. She told me everything, though with difficulty. When she came to know that she was pregnant she got frightened and tried to contact you. That was the time it was rumoured that you were dead in an air crash. Somebody told her so. When she was dismissed from service she got refuge in a convent in Jankpuri, Delhi. They are running an orphanage and clinic. She was under their care till day before yesterday. They admitted her in the government hospital for delivery. While in hospital she saw your photo in the paper, and Came to know about your where about. She took a taxi and came straight to our guard room and asked for you."

They looked at each other in confusion. "She has to be hospitalized immediately" Rukmini said.

"But how I can take her to our hospital. The gynecologist in our hospital is the same lady doctor who was in Ludhiana hospital. Jainamma was her patient when we were in Ambala. Last month, she got transferred here. Whenever she sees me, she asks about Jainamma. How can I take Elamma to her.? What explanation would I give"? Enasu told.

"Why can't we take Elamma to Agarwal hospital in Gurgaon." Rajasekharan suggested.

Agarwal hospital in Gurgaon was run by Dr. Agarwal a retired Govt.Medical College gynecologist. The hospital was very famous for their maternity treatments. For any complicated delivery Agrawal hospital was the answer. Dr. Agarwal deal with infertility cases also. Two years ago, Rajasekharan had a consultation with Dr. Agarwal for Rukmini.

"Sir, I don't have any magic medicine to treat a lady living alone without her husband. You start living together and then come to me if you have any problem. Sleeping with her only during your leave time is not as good as living together." That was his advice.

Agarwal hospital was known for their abortion related service. Any pregnant patient at any age was admitted in Agarwal Hospital. No question was asked. An average of ten abortions were done daily in there. From school girls to housewives of prominent citizens were confidentially admitted there for abortions. Growth of fetus was not a problem, only money mattered. Abortion after four months was considered to be homicide and a criminal offence. But, if the life of a patient is in danger due to the fetus, it could be removed, that was the law. Dr. Agrawal used this law as a loophole to abort even fully matured fetus.

"I am cleaning the nation from illicit children" This was the justification given by the money minded doctor.

Elamma was taken to Agarwal hospital in Rajasekharan's car. Rajasekharan drove the car. Enasu sat in the front seat. Elamma was made to lie downin the back seat resting her head on Rukmini's lap.

Elamma was groaning unconsciously throughout the journey from the quarters to Agarwal hospital. Rukmini caressed her head sympathetically and affectionately. Rukmini was weeping silently at that time.

## 13. War hero returns

The arrangements at the reception area of Agarwal Hospital was superior to any five-star private hospital in the city.

When Rajasekharan's car stopped in front of the "casualty" of the hospital, two attenders in white uniform, rushed towards the Car with a stretcher trolley. Elamma was transferred to the trolley and rushed to examination room. Unlike other hospitals, they started the clinical examinations without enquiring anything to who brought the patient. Until and unless an advance remittance is made in the patient's name, Private hospitals would never attend new cases.

Dr. Agarwal personally examined the patient. He went to his consulting room and called Enasu and Rajasekharan. Rukmini also followed them. They were invited to be seated in front of the doctor. He opened a new file and started to write in it.

"What is the name of patient." Doctor asked.

Enasu said the name and then age.

"When was her last menstruation.?"

Enasu looked at Rajasekharan in wonder.

"We don't know doctor." Rajasekharan said helplessly.

"How is she related to you?" Doctor looked at their faces

"She is my wife's sister." Enasu replied.

"Her husband."?

"Not yet married"

"Oh...I See." Doctor understood the situation.

"Any claims from anyone.?"

"No."

"Any complaint from her side."

"No."

"Look...gentlemen...This is a complicated case. A caesarean would be necessary. The patient is very weak and dehydrated. It is a risky and complicated case and it will be expensive too."

"Money is not a problem doctor."

"That I understand. It appears that you are from Air Force and for you, money won't be a problem." He said with a greedy smile.

Enasu noticed a price list displayed on the wall.

Abortion - normal Rs. 100/- only.

Growth above 60 days. Rs. 150/-

Above 90 days - Rs. 500/-

Caesarean - Rs. 1000/-

Enasu kept two one thousand rupee notes in front of the doctor and murmured. "Doctor, we are not concerned about the child. In fact, the child could be a threat and burden to her and the family since, it was conceived by an illicit relationship. We want her to be saved without any problem."

Rukmini overheard what Enasu had murmured to the doctor. She got angry and jumped to her feet. She removed her gold bangles from her wrist and placed it in front of the doctor. "Doctor, this is my child. My baby. It's a God given gift to me. I will rear the child. I will take care of the mother and child. I want both of them alive and safe. They are mine...." She burst out and cried.

All were shocked. Enasu was afraid to look at her face.

Doctor got up from the chair and left the room. The bangles and notes were untouched. Rajasekharan took them both, gave the notes to Enasu and bangles to Rukmini.

That evening Elamma delivered a male child. It was cesarean. The child was very unhealthy and feeble. Unfortunately, Elamma did not survive. She breathed her last in the labour room.

Enasu paid two thousand rupees to Dr. Agarwal and got a certificate that stated Elamma died of abdominal cancer. She was under his treatment as an inpatient in Agarwal Hospital. Doctor made arrangements to get the police clearance certificate to take the body by flight to Cochin. Then everything became easy for Enasu.

The very next day Enasu telephoned Jainamma.

Usually, Enasu used to call Jainamma every weekend from the hospital but, he never told her about the plane crash and details relating to his injury. She was told that, he was undergoing a special training till August and soon after the training he would take her and child to Delhi to live in the new quarters allotted to them.

Jainamma was waiting for his routine call.

"Jainamma, dear there are two bad news I want to tell you. Please don't get upset. I will be coming tomorrow by flight". Enasu said over phone in a cool voice.

Jainamma giggled and said "Oh...is that a bad news? I was waiting to hear that news for that past six months. Here our natives and the entire people will be thrilled if I tell them that you are coming tomorrow. Our parish priest said he would arrange a grand reception in church for you..." Jainamma continued giggling happily.

"That is not the bad news I wanted to tell you."

"Then...?"

"Jainamma I was admitted in the hospital for the last eight months. Yesterday, I got discharged from the hospital. I was not undergoing special training. I was under treatment."

"Treatment?" Jainamma asked in bewilderment.

"Yes, during the war on December thirteenth night my Aircraft got hit by Pakistani missile. Aircraft crashed. I had to bailout. Luckily I fell very near to our boundary fence. Otherwise they would have put me in Pakistani Jail. "

Jainamma could not believe what she had heard. It was like listening to a story through radio. Her mouth dried. Her head became numb for some time.

"Why didn't you tell me about all this? Oh my God. That was the bravery all papers were praising about? What is the injury? Was it serious?"

"Yes, my left knee was broken. Luckily my leg did not get amputated. They replaced my knee cap with an artificial, imported one."

"Oh... my God..." She cried aloud uncontrollably... she was whimpering for some time.

"How are you now...? Can you walk?" She asked in between her cries.

"Oh yes I am perfectly alright now. I can walk, run, and play. Only thing there is a slight limp while I walk. Otherwise I am perfect..."

"Oh my God... I want to see you darling. I want to see you immediately." She cried again.

"I will be reaching there tomorrow by evening. But..."

"What about then…?"

"There is another bad news. You have to be strong enough to listen. You must console Papa..."

"What is that? Tell me." She was anxious.

"Our Elamma"

"Elamma.? What happened to her...?"

"She is no more."

"What? What are you talking Enasu?"

"She had an abdominal cancer and was in hospital for four months. She never told anyone. Not even telephoned me."

"Cancer?"

"Yes Jainamma. God was very cruel to her. She died yesterday in Hospital. Tomorrow I am coming with her dead body."

A big cry was heard from the other end of the phone.

The phone slipped off from her hand and it was hanging in its wire. Enasu heard the commotion and turmoil at the house through the phone.

"The war hero returns home with dead body of his sister." was the main news in almost all local newspapers next day.

The news spread like wildfire. Being a military nurse Elamma also might had been inflicted with injury from the warfield and might had undergone treatment just like Enasu. Enasu survived. But God took away Elamma's life.

Enasu's air crash and his injury was elaborately narrated in papers. The glorified story of War Hero had diminished the importance of Elamma's death.

At Cochin Airport there was a huge crowd waiting for Enasu. People received him with and boquets and garlands. All were eager to look at the war hero, not at the coffin he had brought along with.

During funeral, the crowd surrounded him. There was a detailed press conference in the parish hall immediately after the funeral, organized by the parish priest. All were proud of their War Hero. All ears were eager to listen to his stories.

"When I sent my daughter along with you, I was relieved as you were with her for her protection and care. But you have returned her to me in a coffin..."

The cry of Raphel pierced through Enasu's heart like sharp arrow.

Raphel's instincts told him that there was something wrong and Enasu was hiding something. This made him worried and depressed.

## 14. Blossoming family

Enasu reached Delhi with Jainamma and their child Ancy. Climate at Delhi was very pleasant. The month of October was the most suitable time to visit North India. The nature was preparing herself to receive the upcoming winter. Rajasekharan and Rukmini were at the airport to receive them. Rukmini was holding their two months old child Unnikrishnan in her arms covered with soft mohair woollen shawl.

Jainamma and Rukmini were meeting for the first time and both of them liked each other. Enasu was holding Ancy in his arms. Jainamma was carrying an airbag with her. She kept the bag down on the floor and took Unnikrishnan in her arms. She felt the child was underweight and looked feeble and sick.

Weight of the child was the first topic of discussion among the two ladies. Unnikrishnan was weighing only three and a half kilogram which was way below the required standard weight of a two-month old child. Ancy was a chubby child and she was weighing nine kilograms which was higher than the required weight of a six-month old child.

Jainamma and Rukmini became intimate friends very quickly. Later they lived like sisters, and their adjacent quarters became one home for them. Rukmini was very talkative and she had a lot to share with Jainamma. Her childhood, adolescent age pre-marriage intimacy with Rajasekharan, pregnancy, delivery, all were referred to one after another in her non stop blabbering.

"Pre-marriage love, was not in my line. I can't think of pre-marriage intimacy at all. It's a sort of sexual fooling around." Said Jainamma said and she thought of her sister Elamma.

"It was not like that; I was the "Murappenu" for Rajan. That means, I was his pre-determined official bride. There were no restrictions for us to express and share our intimacies with each other. In fact, it was our right. Ever since I became mature we were in physical intimacy." Rukmini confessed, shyly.

"My God! It is sin for us. We are Christians. I can't even think of it." Jainamma expressed her shock.

"Forget about the sin part of it. For me that is not an issue. It had an adverse effect on my pregnancy on a later stage." There was a regret in her voice.

"What happened."? Jainamma became anxious.

"I had taken a lot of contraceptive pills to avoid pregnancy before marriage. After the marriage I was not getting conceived. Doctor said It was due to over consumption of contraceptive pills. I had to take lot of medicines to conceive. Those over medication had an adverse effect on my baby. The child was only one and a half kilogram when he was born. The size of the child was of a kitten."

Jainamma felt sorry for the child.

"Everybody thought the child would be lost. The child was in incubator for a month. My poor child, he was fed with bottle milk. My breasts did not have milk at all. The milk producing glands in my breasts got dried due to the adverse effect of the medicines. My poor child is destined to take only bottle milk, not breast feed." Rukmini made up a convincible story and presented it well.

"By the grace of God I have plenty of milk in my breasts. Sometimes I have to milk out some by myself to get relief from swelling and pain." Jainamma said, and what she said was true.

The next day both the ladies were sitting on a sofa side by side in Enasu's quarters, feeding their babies. Jainamma was feeding from her breast and Rukmini from the feeding bottle.

Ancy sucked in sufficient milk swiftly and started dozing. The excessively sucked milk not gulped was flowing out through the corner of her mouth. Unnikrishnan was struggling to suck the rubber nipple of the milk bottle. By chance the child happened to see the milk drop leaked at the protruded nipple of the swelled breast of Jainamma through the corner of his eyes. Suddenly the infant spit out the rubber nipple from his mouth, He turned his head and extended his tiny arms toward Jainamma's breast with a loud cry.

It was an outburst of the suppressed urge for the breast feed of the child. Jainamma could realize the feeling of the infant. Immediately she lifted Ancy from her lap and laid her on the sofa. She was already asleep. Jainamma picked up the crying Unnikrishnan from Rukmini's lap, kept him on hers, and pushed the nipple of her breast into the child's mouth.

The child sucked her nipple with all his might and started feeding. He shook his legs vigorously as an expression of triumph and Joy.

A divine smile appeared on Jainamma's face. But Rukmini started to weep, without any reason, and she was not knowing why for she was weeping.

Later, that became a routine affair. Whenever Unnikrishnan was hungry Rukmini took him to Jainamma, and she fed him till his stomach was full.

When the child started crawling, baby Unnikrishnan would crawl himself through the veranda and reach up to Enasu's quarters. He would bang on the front door, if it was closed. Jainamma was happy to have the child in her lap and fed him just like a mother would.

Even after stopping breast feed for Ancy, Jainamma continued to feed Unnikrishnan till the child reached up to fourteen months of age. Unnikrishnan had gained health and weight only because of Jainamma's breast feeding. She had fed him further, until she would have got the placement as a teacher in Air Force High School. New Delhi, after six months.

Unnikrishnan had two mothers. A mother to feed him and another to rear. He had one more mother, the delivered mother. and that was known to only three persons in the world. They were Enasu, Rajasekharan and Rukmini.

## 15. Drastic disaster

January 26th is celebrated as the Republic day of India. The whole of India was celebrating with wide varieties of programme. Republic day parade, at Delhi, is a colorful ceremonial event. The most wonderful Parade is followed by several cultural programme including folk dances and floats from each state.

The entire Air force camp was very busy on that day. Unnikrishnan's birthday was also on the same day. Jainamma was the headmistress of Air Force High School, and she had to prepare the school children to be lined up at 'Rajpath' to witness the parade as per the Government order. She left the house early in the morning, even without having her breakfast.

Not only Unnikrishnan and Ancy, the other children of Joby and Sabu also were to witness the parade.

Rajasekharan went for duty as he was the flight commander of the Aircraft formation that led the fly past over the Rajpath at the time of Parade; followed by aerobatics which would be the thrilling event of all the programmes. Being the Air Traffic Controller Enasu alsowould be at ATC well in advance. Both the families lived like one big family, even though they lived in separate quarters side by side. On that day, Rukmini and Jainamma had decided to serve rice gruel with pickle and curd, for breakfast. Most of the days both the families had food at Rajasekharan's dining room. Rukmini was in charge of the kitchen, since Jainamma was busy with her school activities.

Enasu never liked rice gruel. He always wanted to have something sumptuous for breakfast. So both men decided to have their breakfast from outside.

Soon after breakfast, the children went to school. Joby and Sabu had their cycles to go to school where as, Ancy and Unnikrishnan had their own Scooters. Rukmini had to accompany Jainamma in the school bus to Rajpath to witness the parade. Usually parents were not allowed to travel in school buses. As Jainamma was the headmistress of the school she had the privilege to take Rukmini with her.

The Parade was very colourful and a majestic one. The fly past and the aerobatics, by fighter aircrafts were thrilling and the show was mind boggling. The daring performance of the pilots were spectacular. Rukmini was very proud to see her husband lead the flight formations.

"You should have flown two hundred feet more down. I had directed you to fly at three hundred feet altitude. But you were at six hundred. If you had flown at three hundred, the VIP's on the dais would have pissed in their pants." Enasu told Rajasekharan, when he later went to ATC to meet him after the fly past exercise. He had parked his aircraft at Palam tarmac. Other aircrafts were flown to their original base at Agra.

"Further lowering of altitude would be dangerous. Fifty per cent of the spectators were school children. Even nursery school children were there. They would be frightened." Rajasekharan justified.

"Hey Enasu. Now the time is ten thirty. I did not have my breakfast. Not even a cup of coffee. My stomach is growling, let's go and have something from the canteen." Rajasekharan said. He looked tired.

"Go where? to the Canteen? At this time? You won't even get biscuits from there."

"Then why don't we go home and have something."

"There won't be anybody at home. Both the ladies will return only after the crowd has dispersed. They have a tea party at school, that's what I heard. It will be about twelve when they return home."

"Don't bother, I will make egg bulls eye and bread toast. We will have a beer too. Today, we need not go to our sections. Let us also celebrate the holiday." Rajasekharan suggested.

"That is a fine idea. Let us go home then."

Both left the Air Traffic control Tower and drove in Enasu's jeep to their quarters at South Block.

The entire AirForce camp was deserted. All were at Rajpath witnessing the cultural programme, and road shows, after the parade.

They reached the quarters. Unnikrishnan's scooter was seen parked in front of Enasu's quarters.

"That bloody scoundrel Unni has bunked the show programs. In fact, he was very fond of folk dances, then why did he skip?" Rajasekharan wondered.

The front door was closed. Enasu picked up the key from his pocket. The door was not locked. He pushed the door and entered the house. Rajasekharan followed him.

Enasu heard some unusual sounds from his bed room. The bedroom door was closed. He pushed open the door.

He was shocked and horrified when he saw a dreadful sight inside. With all his might he cried aloud. "Oh...My God.... Raja. Look!"

His frantic voice was very fierce.

Rajasekharan ran to him and looked inside over his shoulders.

He saw Unnikrishnan and Ancy were struggling to get out of bed. Both were naked!

Ancy got panicked, she could not pick up her under clothes from the floor. She grabbed her top in a hurry and ran to the toilet and slammed the door shut. Unnikrishnan hid behind the dressing table.

With a violent cry Enasu fell on the sofa. His voice was so hoarse and loud. His face had a fierce look.

Rajasekharan was afraid that someone would listen to his loud roar and come running to find out what was happening. Luckily none was nearby. All were at the parade.

"Enasu, please calm down. Calm down. Please don't fuss up the situation. I am also equally shocked and frustrated. Please bear with me. Somehow need to solve the issue, don't we...? Calm down..."

Rajasekharan consoled him calmly. But he was also shivering.

"What will I do Raja? I am ruined. I will kill both of them and kill myself."

He uttered like a madman and banged on his chest violently with his own fist. Rajasekharan had to exert force to stop him from hitting.

He let Enasu cry out for some time. Slowly his violent cry subsided and turned to be a sob with whimpering became silent, but was panting heavily.

Rajasekaran sat by the side of his friend and patted his back affectionately and sympathetically. He also was in utter confusion, not knowing what to do further.

It was a great blow to both of them. They never expected such an act from their children. They had forgotten that their children had grown up. It was their duty to put a barrier between the adolescent boy and girl. They were playing together, eating together, sometimes sleeping together just like in their childhood. They grew up together as a family and no one expected them to be in this kind of a relationship.

Everything went out of hand. Now what can be done? How to resolve the issue? Both became very upset. Their hearts were burning in agony.

Unnikrishnan dressed himself in pants, shirt and a sweater over it, he stood before them very calmly. He didn't look worried or tensed. He was very cool.

"Acha, Dad", he addressed both Rajasekharan and Enasu, "I know, what we have done is not right. But we love each other and want to get married!"

Enasu did not allow him to talk further. He jumped to his feet to slap Unnikrishnan's face. But Rajasekharan caught hold of his hand."

Enasu shouted aloud..." No No....No... You bloody fool."

"Why Dad...? Why can't I marry Ancy...? Because I am a Hindu?" Unnikrishnan asked very boldly.

"No... Not that..." Answered Rajasekharan.

"Then, why not? Ancy loves me; and I love her. We are already twenty years old, we have the right to take our own decision. "Unnikrishnan argued sternly.

"No. You can't marry her." Rajasekharan said again firmly.

"Why not.? I am asking you why not?" Unnikrishnan raised his voice. And his voice was harsh.

He had never raised his voice in front of his father ever before. His body language was also unusual and rebellious, which was very new to Enasu and Rajasekharan.

At this juncture, Rajasekharan was compelled to reveal the truth to him. The truth about his paternity.

"Ancy is your own sister...... Unni. You are this great man Enasu's son. I am only your foster father. Your Amma, Rukmini is not your own mother. She was infertile. Therefore, we had to adopt you."

Rajasekharan, somehow managed to tell that much.

He was breathing very hard as if he walked miles.

"What are you talking Acha? There must be some logic even if you bluff. Me and Ancy are same age though she is four months oider than me. Mummy could never have delivered another child in four months' gap, Can she?" Unnikrishnan argued, although he was confused.

"You were not delivered by Jainamma. You were delivered by her sister Elamma. But Your father is Enasu, the same father of Ancy. Both of you are his children. Now is it clear.?" Rajasekharan said bluntly.

It was like bomb explosion for Unnikrishnan. The bomb exploded right in his heart. He felt as if the entire glands in his body were burning. His eyes became blurry. Some sort of howling sound was echoing in his ears. He felt his body became weightless. He lost his balance and fell forward, hitting his forehead very hard on the wooden hand rest of sofa. The fall was very fierce. His forehead was injured with a deep cut. Blood started to ooze out.

Enasu and Rajasekharan were shocked and stunned. They stood motionless for sometime.

Enasu tried to lift Unnikrishnan in his arms. It was difficult for him to lift sixty Kilogram alone. Both of them jointly took him and ran towards their jeep, parked in front of the house.

Ancy was hiding inside the bath room. She was shivering like a wet kitten. She had heard her father shout and heard a loud cry, probably from Unnikrishnan. Dad might have beaten him, she thought.

When all sounds subsided a dreadful silence followed. She opened the bathroom door a little and peeped through.

There was no one in the room. She came out of the bathroom, picked up her pants from underneath the cot, dressed quickly and went to the front room. No-body was there. She went to her own room and lay flat on the bed, and cried.

By twelve Jainamma and Rukmini reached home and found the front door was ajar. When they entered inside Jainamma noticed blood stains on the floor, with black ants on it.

"Oh... my God. Rukmini, look here. See what is this? My God! It is blood. A pool of blood." She was frightened. Ancy came out of her room as if she was fast asleep. She also saw the blood. Dad might have beaten Unni. They might have taken him to hospital! She was frightened.

"Ancy, what is this? How did blood get in here? This is not your period time."

"I don't know mummy. I was taking bath when they were talking?"

"Who were talking?"

"Dad, Acha and Unni. I heard dad was shouting at Unni. Acha might have beaten him. I heard him crying too. I was inside the bathroom."

Ancy and her siblings addressed Enasu as Dad and Rajasekharan as Acha, same as that Unnikrishnan, addressed.

Just in time, Enasu called from the hospital. He said while jumping over the sofa Unnikrishnan had a fall and got an injury on his forehead. He lost some blood. There were three stitches. He may have to be hospitalized for two days. He asked Jainamma to pack one or two shirts and pants for Unnikrishnan and keep it ready. He would come soon and pick it up.

"Why did he jump over the Sofa...?" She asked.

"There was an argument between Raja and Unni, on some silly issue. He raised his hand to beat Unni. He was trying to escape by jumping over the Sofa. And fell." Enasu explained.

Jainamma suspected something fishy might have happened. But she could not figure out what it was.

## 16. Advaita Ashram

Unnikrishnan's conscience was deeply hurt and he was mentally dejected and depressed. He regretted over having misled and abused his own sister, though unknowingly. It was the biggest sin. Such grave mistakes would never be forgiven or forgotten.

"What would be my destiny? "Unnikrishnan got afraid. He was frightend of the future outcome of the blunder.

Another great blow was the revelation of his paternity. All of a sudden he became an illegitimate son. Disgusting and shameful.

He had three stitches on his forehead above the left brow and was advised to be hospitalized for a few days. His mental agony was far deeper than his physical injury.

Unnikrishnan embraced his father and foster father together. He embraced them both and cried very loudly. His cry was heard at distance and people from other wards gathered in front of his room. They stood peeping through windows and doors which made Enasu to become embarrassed. Rajasekharan also got upset. Even after weeping for a longer time. Unnikrishnan did not loose his grip around his father. They had to exert force to release his hold. On hearing his loud cry, Medical Officer on duty rushed to the room and gave him a sedative injection. Suddenly his limbs became feeble and Unnikrishnan slept like a child.

That evening when Jainamma and Rukmini visited Unnikrishnan, he reacted in the same way; he hugged them tightly and started crying hysterically. Both the ladies also cried along with him. Enasu and Rajasekharan found it difficult to console the ladies. At last Rajasekharan compelled them to leave the room. Unnikrishnan repeated the same mischievous behaviour with Joby and Sabu also.

However, when Ancy went near to him, his attitude changed, he was furious, his eyes reddened.

He looked at her with widened wild eyes, his facial expression looked beastly and mean. He lifted his left leg and kicked her buttock. Ancy fell down and cried.

He roared at her. "Never come to me...never...never..."

He was panting heavily for a long time. He had to be sedated again.

It turned out to be a big shock to Ancy. They were together ever since they were born. They grew up together and lived together all those years. It was only very recently, their close relationship enticed them, which eventually turned into an obsession. Intentionally or unintentionally Unnikrishnan happened to touch Ancy's breast. Initially it was taken lightly but one led to another and they started becoming physically attracted to each other. An unknown eagerness developed in between them to know each other more. An eagerness for sexual intimacy developed from within. They forgot themselves in the influence of love and lust. And lust overpowered love.

Ancy felt hurt when she saw the hatredness in Unnikrishnan's wide eyes.

"Sir, I am afraid that the fall has affected his brain. The impact of the fall might have affected his cognition and behavior. The unsteadiness in his behavior proves that." The medical officer told Rajasekharan very confidentially.

Rajasekharan looked at his face, with fear and anxiety.

"I suggest you better take him to our MH (Military Hospital) and show him to Dr. Cherian the Psychiatrist, He is an expert. Let him diagnose. I will refer the case to him." He said.

Rajasekharan became very upset. Unnikrishnan was his only son. For him Unnikrishnan was born to him. Never thought otherwise. His son was his life. The child had given him and Rukmini a life. Both of them were living for him. He was a brilliant and intelligent boy. An extraordinary type. He was the only student from St. Xaviers's College to get selected for medicine in the campus selection conducted by All India Institute of Medical Sciences. Getting admission in AIIMS was nearly impossible. He had to join by April first week. Only three months left. If he happened to have any brain problem as suspected by the medical officer, It would take months for him to recover, if at all he did recover from the trauma.

Rajasekharan fell like crying, after listening to the doctor's opinion.

When Enasu came to know what doctor had said, he got annoyed. "*That* Medical officer is an idiot. What he said was utter nonsense. If at all he has some brain problem a neurologist is to be consulted and not a bloody psychiatrist. But I don't suspect anything of that sort. He is all shaken up and distressed. He is feeling guilty about his actions and he is yet to comprehend everything we told him. I think he will recover soon and come in terms with the situation, if we extend our full support, care and love. It will greatly benefit him, if we arrange a good counselling session for him".

Rajasekharan looked at Enasu for some time and said. "If you don't get annoyed, I will suggest a good place where he can get a very good counselling".

"Why should I get annoyed? To get him a best counselling session is our problem. For that any devils den is acceptable for me". Then we will take him to Swamy Jnanananda.He is a deity."

"You know very well Raja, that I don't believe in temple, church rituals and the deity business.

But you can't just call that place a temple; it's a house of wisdom and peace".

"Which is the place you are talking about?"

"Advaita Ashram in North Delhi. Near river Yamuna..."

"Yes... I know that place. It is a den of fanatic Hindus."

"Oh... No. Not at all. It is an educational institution, a spiritual school. It is a big campus of more than ten acres, spread out up to the bank of river Yamuna. They teach the concept of Dharma, theism, and ideals of moksha and salvation, based on Bhagavad Gita. The Ashram was started on the basis of Advaita Vadanda by Swamy Chinmayananda Saraswathy".

"Advaita Vedanda.... Swamy Chinmayananda?" I think I have heard of him"

"Chinmayananda Saraswathy was a guru and a spiritual leader who died recently in Chicago. His original name was Balakrishna Menon from our place Kerala. That too from Ernakulam. He was a spiritual leader who inspired the formation of Chinmayananda mission a worldwide non-profit organisation to spread the knowledge of Advaita Vedanda. "

"What is this Advaita Vedanda? "Enasu was inquisitive to know more.

"It is a spiritual theory?"

"What is that?"

"Paramathma or the supreme soul can be considered as a metaphysical energy, which is the power of nature. According to Advaita, there is no distinction between souls, there is only one soul, all lives originate from it and end up in it and that is the concept." "If we put into Christian version, the Holy spirit and our soul is one."

"So?"

"The salvation is the peace of mind when you are alive, and not after death. They are not teaching about the eternal life after death.... but about ...how to live in peace till the death. The head of the Ashram is Swamy Jnanananda. Jnanananda means one rejoices in the wisdom. He is a European. He was a Christian priest once, and a professor in Oxford. Somehow, he met swamy Chinmayanadnda and became his follower. He is also a guru to many followers."

"How do you know him? I was in Delhi for the last twenty years and I have never heard of such a fellow."

"Every day morning All India Radio is broadcasting a programme." 'Today's thought and tomorrows guide'. Swamy is one of the preachers."

"Oh...that early morning nuisance bla...bla..." Enasu showed ridiculous gesture with his lips.

"Don't ridicule when you don't know the subject."

"OK...OK... Anyway it is not in my line. You want us to take Unnikrishnan to Advaita Ashram?" There was a sense of dislike and disagreement in his face and voice.

"Exactly. That is my suggestion."

"Will they make him mad by over chanting and preaching?"

"Believe me Enasu, Advaita Ashram is governed scientifically and psychologically. Not by inducing blind beliefs and orating rituals. They depend on proven reality not on superstitions, Swamy Jnanananda is a psychologist, philosopher and theologist, having wide knowledge in Christian and Hindu doctrines."

"*Does* he lives in the Ashram"

"That's what I heard."

"Then his name will be in the telephone directory."

"May be. It's better to get an appointment."

'Let me see whether I can talk to him over the phone."

They went to hospital reception and asked for the phone directory. Enasu turned the pages.

"Yes. here it is Adwait Ashram. Oh my God! there are ten numbers."

"Dial the first number."

Enasu dialed the first number. A recorded eulogical hindu song was heard as dialer tone. A female voice followed.

"Hello... Advaita Ashram. Peace on you. Who is calling.?"

"This is from Air force Delhi. Can you connect me to swami Jnanananda?" Enasu said in a tough voice.

"May I know what the matter is please?" She asked.

"Hey lady. I will talk about it, only with Swamy Jnanananda." His voice was very harsh. There was a click sound on the other end. After a few seconds a soft voice was heard.

"Hello, I am Jnanananda, sorry for annoying you, sir. My secretary got frightened. But this is our system. All calls will come through her. Can you please tell me whom I am speaking to?"

"*Oh* Good evening sir, sorry swami I am Enasu. Wing commander of Indian Air Force, chief Air traffic controller". Enasu said politely, but his voice was rough.

"Oh... I am honoured to have a V.I.P on line sir. May I know, what do you want from this humble organisation?"

Immediately Enasu said bluntly. "Over humbleness is a sign of pride Swamy".

There was a big laugh at the other end of the phone.

"Tell me sir, what do you want."?

'"I want to meet you."

"For What.?"

"To get some direction from you. Sorry an advice. Now, I am in deep distress. If somebody doesn't help me now, I will be sunk forever." Enasu's eyes become moistened, when he said so.

"When would you like to meet me.?"

*"Is it* possible now. Just now.?"

"Is that urgent?"

"For me it is an emergency."

"OK then I will cancel my scheduled prayer programme."

"My problem is greater than your routine. prayer Swamy."

Again there was loud laugh at the other end.

"Please come sir. I will wait for you." The phone disconnected.

Hey... what sort of a fellow you are? Is it the way to talk to a spiritual leader?" Rajasekharan got annoyed.

"He is really a spiritual man.

That's why he invited me," Enasu smiled.

"You want me to come with you, "

"Not now..."

Enasu ran towards his jeep.

## 17. Advaita Ashram

The main entrance of "Adwaith Ashram" looked like a Hindu pilgrimage centre with lots *of* saffron coloured flags and displayed banners with Bhagavad Gita verses. A big marble statue of Lord Krishna blowing a conch installed on the platform near the gate was very attractive. A clock mounted on the facade of security office indicated the time as 7.45. Since that was winter season, darkness had already set in very early.

When Enasu identified himself, the security guard politely said, "Swamiji is expecting you, sir."

Enasu passed through the main gate. He observed that the scenario inside the compound wall was entirely different from what was expected. There were so many buildings. All the roads were tiled and clean. The entire area was well illuminated with flood lights. All buildings had sign boards fixed in front of them. The first building was a prayer hall. The second was the monastery followed by hostels for monks. There were hostels for men and boys separately. There were playgrounds and courts for different games. The area looked like a residential college campus. He could see young men sitting by the side of the windows either reading or writing. Pin-drop silence prevailed everywhere which showed the high degree of discipline maintained.

There was a big mess hall and a cook's house adjacent to it. He could smell an aroma of good spicy food which made his mouth watering. Then he remembered, that he had not eaten anything after breakfast of two slices of roasted bread and a cup of tea. During lunch time he was anxiously waiting at the hospital varanda for clinical test results of Unnikrishnan. He was worried that his son would end up with brain injury or trauma of some kind.

The odour of food made him very hungry. His stomach growled out of hunger. He was desperately in need of some food and he was mentally and physically exhausted.

Swamy Jnanananda's house was at the far end of the campus by the side of Yamuna river. He parked his jeep in the courtyard of the house. A benz car was parked in the garrage.

He saw the unending and continuous waves of Yamuna river glittering like silver frills by the moon light. The sight was beautiful. The splashing of waves embracing the shore was the only sound he heard and it was very pleasant.

Swamy Jnanananda came out of the office, received the visitor, and guided him to his office.

It was a very big room with lot of books everywhere. There were seven book shelves full of books. There were piles of books by the side of his office table too. A brass name plate was kept on the glass-topped table which read "Swamy Jnanananda. (Dr. James Hurd)"

Swamy Jnanananda was a lean and tall man of about, sixty years of age. He was a white skinned European with lot of wrinkles on his face and forehead: He had a long, white beard reaching up to his chest.

"Your office looks like a library "Enasu commented smiling.

"Yes... Yes, I read a lot. Books are my companions."

Swamy's blue eyes were very sharp. They were scanning Enanu's face and mind.

"I think, officer, you are very hungry now. Look tired also. Will you please come with me to my dining room? Food is already served for you. We will eat something and talk. Just like Jesus Christ taught us "Feed the hungry first, then preach righteousness. A hungry stomach will never digest wisdom."

Enasu was wonderstruck. How did the Swamy guess, his state of hunger in advance? He silently followed Swamy to the adjacent dining room.

It was a beautiful dining room with a big glass-top dining table and eight cushioned straight chairs around.

A bowl full of steaming hot vegetable 'Pulave' (Rice cooked with variety of vegetable and spices just like Chinese fried rice), a bunch of banana in a tray, and a jug full of milk were placed at the centre of the table. Two dinner plates with cutlery by its side, and two water filled glasses were arranged. No waiter or an attender was present there.

"Are you expecting someone to have dinner with you.?" Enasu asked.

"I was expecting you, and I knew you would be tired and hungry." Swamy said smiling.

Enasu was shocked and looked at his face with fright.

"Eight fifteen is our dinner time." Swamy said. "Be at home. Only self service is available here. No one will assist you to eat. "

Enasu considered it as a suggestion to start eating.

No living creature can exist without food. When hungry, nothing in the world would quench the need other than food. A hungry person would never have any other desire other than to eat.

Enasu had never experienced such a craving for food in his whole life. The odour of food had lit a fire in his stomach. His hunger pangs were so intense that, he forgot table manners. With a serving spoon he transferred some food to his plate and started to eat swiftly. Then he noticed Swamy was looking at him with piteous eyes. Enasu felt ashamed and self-pity. His face saddened.

"Don't worry son. I can understand your desperation.

Have a glass of water now." Swamy said sympathetically.

Like an obedient child he drank a glass full of water in one go.

"Now let's pray." Swamy said.

He placed both his hands on the table, palms open. He closed his eyes, bowed his head and started praying loudly.

"Our father in heaven, Holy be thy name thy kingdom of righteousness be spread on earth. Forgive our sins as we forgive. Thank you for giving us our daily food. Save us from the evil of temptation".

Then he started to recite Sanskrit verses, thirty-one of chapter six from 'Bhagavad gita'.

"Sarva - bhuta - sthilam, Yah mam bhajati, ekatvam - asthitah, sarvatha varta - manah api sah - yogi – mayi vartate...."

He maintained the same posture for some more time in silence. Then lifted his head and looked at Enasu. He was looking at Swamy in bewilderment.

"One must pray before he eats. That is the expression of gratitude to God in heaven. You know where the heaven is"? he asked.

Enasu got confused. He kept silent.

"Swamy touched his forehead between the eyes and said." It is here, in our nerve centre. You might be wondering, what I recited in Sanskrit. The meaning is one who beholds me as present in all beings, will be with me as I be within him in all circumstances. Whatever he does, I will be with him."

"Now, have your food..."

Enasu started to eat.

"Pulave' is good for a healthy man like you. For me, I don't eat anything oily. I have a simple and light dinner, consisting of a glass of milk and a fruit."

He took one banana and started to peel watching Enasu eating.

Enasu realised that, Swamy had foreseen his arrival and knew what would be his state of mind and body through his divine power.!!

A hot wave of fear passed through his nerves. He realized that he was sitting in front of a holy man and a psychologist.

Sweat beads appeared on Enasu's brow.

After the dinner, Swamy guided him back to his office room and made him sit opposite him.

"You have not told me your name sir, I forgot to ask you too." Swamy asked.

"Oh, I have told you my name over the phone when we talked", He said in wonder.

"At that time you were emphasising your rank. Not name."

There was a ridicule in Swamy's smile. Enasu felt a bit defamed. He remembered how he had talked to him over the phone. He had put more weight on his rank when he said. 'I am wing commander Enasu."

"I am Enasu swamy "He said very politely.

"Enasu.... hmm..." Swamy closed his eyes and thought for a while and then asked. "You know what is the meaning of Enasu?'

"I don't know swamy. It is the name of someone in Bible." He said.

"Not someone. He was son of Abraham the ancient father of the desert. In English it is Isac. In hebrew it is Isahak. In Malayalam it is Enasu. Meaning is 'laughing man' an apt name for you. The name suits you well. You have a smiling face. But deep inside, you are weeping. Your smile is camouflaging your deep sorrow. Am I right?" He said directly looking at Enasu's eyes.

All of a sudden Enasu's eyes became moistened. He wiped his eyes with handkerchief to stop his tears. But he could not control or stop sobbing. Initially he was weeping silently and later he started crying out loud, covering his face with both hands. He took a couple of minutes to regain his composure. All the while Swamy was just watching him silently.

When he became completely normal. Swamy said.

"Don't worry my son. Everything is going to be alright. Today is your day. God is guiding you to a new sphere of wisdom. It was his decision to bring you here, to unload all your guilt here, to make you free, come on son, what happened?!"

Swamy's voice was very grave and deep. It touched the bottom of his heart.

"Quite unexpectedly I happened to witness my daughter in my bedroom in a very awkward situation". He said looking down. Tear drops rolled down through his cheeks.

"Fornication? "Swamy asked.

"Yes."

"With whom?"

"With my son"

His eyes were again filled with tears, and lips shivered and throat was choked

"What.?"

"But she was not aware that he was her own brother."

"What about that boy?"

"He was also unaware. Now, he knows everything. He is extremely upset and hysterical. He is hospitalized, I don't know what to do now. That's why I am here swamy". Enasu wept again.

Swamy allowed him to weep for some more time. "Tell me my son, who all know that the boy is your son??"

"Me, Rajasekharan and his wife Rukmini. They are his foster parents."

"Your wife?"

"No. She does not know. My daughter doesn't know either."

"Does your friend have any other children?"

"No. Rukmini is infertile."

"Oh.... I see, now tell me...how this all happened. I want to know all about it, right from scratch".

"It is a very big story Swamy. It will take long time to tell."

"Don't worry. All the night is ours" He looked at the digital calendar clock fitted on the wall and said.

Enasu also looked at the clock. The time was 9.45 and the date was 28th Jan.1991.

## 18. The retirement

It was forty minutes past midnight when Enasu finished the narration of his life story. Though it was winter season, and the atmospheric temperature was just below ten degrees, Enasu was sweating... His inner clothes were drenched in sweat. Jnanananda Swamy pushed forward a cup of black coffee towards him and asked him to drink. Enasu sipped the hot coffee and felt relieved. He looked at Swamy gratefully and smiled.

"Thank you, sir" he said.

"God has directed you here, for this very moment."

"To drink black coffee.?"

Swamy liked his joke and he laughed

"No. To get relieved of tension and all the excess baggage you have been carrying all these years."

"Yes... Yes... I feel relieved now." He said.

"I know; you are well relieved. You have poured your heart out. Your mind is cleansed of its past baggage. Now you can fill it up with good thoughts and wisdom. It would be digested quickly."

"In fact, I came here to fix up an appointment with you for a counselling for Rajasekharan's son Unnikrishnan." Enasu said

"Say, Your son." Swamy corrected him. "Yes,..Yes... My son, Unni." Said Enasu.

"In fact, you were in need of a counselling, not your son Unnikrishnan. After all what is counselling? It involves listening to unresolved problems and difficulties of a person and giving necessary advice and guidance to help them overcome or resolve their conflict. That's what is being done here. Now onwards everything will be in order. You are called upon to lead a mass, like David. You know who is David."? Swamy asked.

"David? Is it group Captain David of Western Air Command?"

Swamy laughed loudly. "Oh...No This David was a king... King of Israel. Father of Solomon. A man of wisdom and leader of a dynasty. A legend."

"Yes, I have heard of him, a character in Bible."

"Yes. When he was lifted up from a shepherd upto the throne of the king, he had forgotten the morality. Lust lured him. Later he opened up his heart to God. Repented very vigorously. God lifted him again to lead Israel. You are another David chosen by God. Go peacefully now."

It was a farewell bid.

"You may bring them here, your friend Rajasekharan and your son Unnikrishnan tomorrow. I mean today by 10.30. I will wait for you."

Enasu got up from the chair, went closer to Swamy, bowed in front of him then touched his feet. Swamy placed both his hands over his head and said." God be with you."

Time was one thirty-five past midnight.

"Rajasekharan told me that he would wait for me. He might have slept by now. For the last four days none of us had slept at all." Enasu said while he was walking towards his jeep.

Swamy walked along with him up to the vehicle. "Your son and your friend are still awake. Both of them are waiting for you." Swamy said smilingly. That was another divine vision of Swamy.

Rajasekharan, and Unnikrishnan were waiting on a bench in the varanda of the hospital. Rajasekharan was sitting, and Unnikrishnan was lying, with his head rested on the lap of his Acha. Rajasekharan was caressing Unni's head. When the jeep stopped in front of them on the road, both of them got up to receive Enasu.

Unnikrishnan appeared to be very normal. His face was clear of all unpleasantness. His eyes were clear of sorrow and guilt. Enasu felt that, it was a miracle. He remembered what swamy had said." Now onwards every thing will be in order."

"What happened.? "Enasu asked in wonder.

"I have explained to our son everything. And he understood. Am I right? My son?"

"Yes. Acha. I know everything. I think it is better if no other person knows this. I want my paternity and maternity to be a secret. Now I have two fathers, Acha and Dad. I love you both Acha... Dad."

He put his arms around his Acha and Dad.

"Now there won't be be any problem. That's what swamy told me Raja, he is a Deity a real Deity." Enasu said.

"What did he say?" Rajasekharan asked.

"I revealed my actual life story to him. No, he made me to reveal. He told me to bring you both to his ashram by ten thirty. Now, let's get some sleep. Only a few hours left till dawn."

Rajasekharan and Unnikrishnan slept on the cot. Enasu used the sofa as his bed. All the three slept in no time, as if their sleep was controlled by a switch.

"Everybody on earth has one mother and one father. Whereas you have three mothers and two fathers. One mother to give birth to you. One mother to feed you, and a third mother to take care of you. A trio maternal origin. Very rare and wonderful, isn't it Unnikrishnan?" Swamy asked.

"Yes Swamiji. I am blessed." Unnikrishnan said and smiled.

The three of them, Enasu, Unnikrishnan and Rajasekaran were sitting in front of swami Jnananda in the Ashram.

"You all are blessed, except for your deceased mother, all of you are in a very special and loving relationship. Though Jainamma does not know details of your birth and paternity, she loves you like her son, which is a good thing. Let it go like this, let this secret not go to another person's ear. Never". Swamy advised.

"The immediate action you should take is to separate Unnikrishnan and Ancy, so that they don't see each other hereafter. At least a for few years. Being a girl, Ancy will forget this episode very quickly, as long as she does not know that he is her own brother. If she came to know that Unni is her brother, she will not be able to overcome the shock and may end up in some sort of unstablity.

Let Unnikrishnan stay in this campus, and study for his medicine. Since AIIMS is nearby it will be convenient for him and also, it will help to motivate other children to study, if they have a doctor student with them.

I think it is time for you, Enasu to retire from service and go to your native place. Something big, very big assignment is waiting for you there." Swamy said as if he was looking at the future through his divine vision.

Whatever Swamy Jnanananda had predicted became true later.

Unnikrishnan, became a hosteller of Advaita Ashram, and joined in AIIMS Delhi for his medicine.

Later he choseto wear saffron shirt, and Rudraksha chain, same as that of other inmates of the hostels in the Ashram, He was known as 'Doctor Swamy'.

Enasu voluntarily retired from Air force and settled at Kakkanadukara, in Vazhakkala Bungalow. Ancy got her admission in Alleppy Medical College. Joby and Sabu joined in Maharaja's college, where their father had studies.

Enasu spent more time in studying the comparison of Bible and Bhagavad gita at Advaita Ashram at Cochin.

# Part 2

## 19. The great fall

Enasu retired from Air force after thirty years of service. He was fifty years old then. He was very active. He did not want to live an idle retired life.

Devassy, his father was seventy-seven years old and he was getting tired day by day. However, he was not sick. His eyesight and hearing were perfect.

"Oh my son. It is good that you left the service and have come home. I am aged now. You may take over the plantation and whatever wealth we have. Our family has one hundred and fifty acres of plantation, developed by your grandfather. After the partition now we are left with thirty-eight acres." Devassy said to his son.

"Appa, I am not interested in plantation and agriculture. That won't suit me. I want to do some business and become an industrialist." Enasu expressed his desire.

"It is a wonderful idea. In that case you may sell off some land and utilize that fund for your industry." His father gave him the consent.

"Enasu's children, Ancy, Jobby and Sabu were thrilled to be at their native place and to live in their ancestral house with their dear granddad.

Jainamma was also happy for having settled in the native place.

"Now I am happy. I can peacefully close my eyes forever; I was waiting for this day." said Devassy.

"No Appa. Your time is not yet over. I want you to live and bless the marriage of my children". Enasu said from his heart.

It so happened as Enasu wished, Devassy lived for seven more years and was blessed to see all his grandchildren getting married. He was also lucky to see his great grandchild, Ancy's baby.

Enasu made a sea of changes in the plantation area. He made it as a township. He cut off all the rubber trees and sold the land as small housing plots. Within five years, the entire valley was filled with hundreds of houses. A new road was developed just near to Vazhakkala house. The entire area was known as Vazhakkala, and it became the northern area of city.

In collaboration with a Japanese company Enasu started a new industrial venture at the far end of Vazhakala area.

Starting of an industry by a retired air force officer was welcomed by the Government. He had received financial support and assistance from The Industrial Development Corporation, to start the factory, PLPB Ltd.

Enasu's project was manufacturing of "Poly Laminated Paper Boards". Raw materials used were old newspapers. All the machinery required for the production of boards were imported from China. The process of manufacturing board was fully automatic. Old newspaper soaked in water proof and fire proof synthetic gum was spread over the drier mat of the machine. Layers will be added as per the required thickness of the board. The gum soaked layered paper stock would then pressed hydraulically and dried to form the board. Both the sides of the board would be laminated with colored polycarbonate thin sheet. Making the multi colored board, water, fire and termite proof.

Quality of PLPB board was superior to any other board that was available in the market.

Total project cost was thirty million Indian rupees. In 1994 that was a very huge amount. PLPB Ltd was considered to be one of the best medium sector companies of Kerala. PLPB boards captured overseas market. When they received export orders, the profile of the company along with the photo of Enasu, were appeared in almost all news papers.

There were two hundred employees working in the factory. They were all well paid. They were well disciplined too. Within five years PLPB became one of the leading industrial units in Cochin, and a major exporter of Poly Laminated Paper Boards in Kerala.

Ancy completed her MBBS degree and also passed PG in ophthalmology medicine. She was married to Dr. Jose from Kottayam, an ENT specialist, and both of them had started a clinic in Dubai. They had two daughters.

Joby took B. Tech degree and joined in PLPB Ltd to help his father in production and running of the factory. He was staying with his father at Vazhakkala house. He got married and had two children.

Sabu became an MBA Graduate, and was looking after the marketing of PLPB Ltd. He was very fond of gardening. He took diploma in horticulture from Singapore Horticulture College. He made beautiful gardens in factory and Vazhakkala house.

He stayed in a beautiful house near the banks of Periyar river with his wife and a child. Exporting of fresh flowers was his main hobby.

The Chairman & Managing Director VD Enasu became a celebrity, not because he was an industrialist and a very rich man, but he was known as a writer, philosopher, and an orator too. The book written by Enasu 'The salvation' had received wide range of publicity and criticism. He wrote about God and his faith. He was a blind believer of God. But his belief had different dimensions.

"God is the inherent power of nature, creator of the entire universe. God is the omnipotent and benevolent, having ultimate power to create, govern and if necessary destroy. Christ called that power as "Abba", Nabi called "Allah". Vedas proclaimed as "Eswar or Bhagavan". Whatsoever is the name, it is one and the same. God uses destructive power against one who stands against his law. His law is Righteousness. To form different religions man gave different names for God. All that are fictional. Rituals are fictional. Life originates from the power of nature and returns to nature its origin"

There is no heaven and hell after death. Both are the states of mind. No one can approach God or please God by rituals and offerings. God is within us. Meditation is the only way to communicate with God, we can hear his voice in our mind while meditating...."

Enasu was invited to attend seminars and religious conferences and convocations. People listened to him very attentively. So many were attracted to his theory of God and salvation.

It was Enasu's sixtyeth birth day, the civilian authorities and the company staff jointly arranged a reception. A dais and podium was erected in the football ground of the factory. About five hundred people including invitees were seated as audience. When Enasu was garlanded and escorted to the dias a loud applause was echoed. Lady staff presented a welcome song which was very much appealing to the crowd. After a few felicitations Enasu got up and moved towards the podium to deliver his speech. The audience was eager to listen to the philosopher.

Even at sixty, Enasu was looking very energetic and smart. He stood tall at six feet, with proportionally built healthy body. He wore a light blue colored safari suit. His grey hair was trimmed short. He had a clean shaved flat cheeked face. His face was very peaceful, eyes were very sharp and his look was very authoritative.

He talked very slowly through the microphone. His sound was heavy, but each word was clearly heard.

He expressed his gratitude to the staff and municipal authorities for organizing the felicitation.

Then he said "gratitude is a part of righteousness stipulated in the holy books".

His tone was very serious and the body language was that of a teacher.

"There are two holy books I always refer. Bible and Bhagavad Gita. Both are same for me. ...Bible talks about righteousness, Gita talks about Dharma and both are same."

He wanted to say something further, but suddenly his face became pale. The mic which he was holding dropped from his hand. With both hands he pressed his chest as if he had a darting pain. His eyes rolled back and he fell on the ground face down.

The audience jumped to their feet. There was a big commotion and cry. Shrill voices of the ladies from the audience were heard at a very long distance. They rushed to their chairman. The General Manager Thampy and the Works Manager Rajan, both were very hefty and heavily built men. They lifted Enasu in their arms and ran towards the road. By the time the company ambulance was placed at the spot.

The ambulance roared and rushed to the Medical College Hospital with its siren and head lights flashing, which the crowed looked on with shock and horror.

## 20. ICCU another world

"If you were late, even by three minutes to bring Enasu here, his heartbeat would have stopped forever". The Cardiologist came out and spoke to the crowd gathered in the courtyard of the Medical College Hospital, Ernakulam.

There were sighs of relief amongst the crowd. Some factory employees raised their voice and thanked God. They were afraid that their chairman Enasu had passed away. That's what they heard.

Enasu was not just a chairman of the company for them. He was their teacher, mentor, protector and guardian. They loved him sincerely. His demise would have been unbearable for them.

While everyone was relieved by the good news, one among them stood perplexed. That was Thampy Swamy, the General Manager of the factory.

From the very inception of the factory, Thampy Swamy was in charge of personal management and overall control of labor. He hails from a Brahmin family from Palakkad, but he married a Christian lady and had two grown up daughters. Though he was very sincere in his profession, being over proactive and over enthusiastic he always ended up in troubles.

He accompanied Enasu in the ambulance along with works manager Rajan. Rajan was sitting in the front seat along with the driver while Thampy was sitting beside Enasu, holding his boss's hand.

He was caressing Enasu's hand out of care and respect, throughout the journey to the hospital. He had to try very hard to control his tears and sob due to his devotion and love towards his boss Enasu.

While caressing his boss's hand, he did not feel the pulse in his wrist. He was shocked and upset. He checked and checked again. There was no pulse. He pressed his palm over his chest and checked for the heartbeat. He did not feel anything. But the body was warm.

He expressed his apprehension and concern to Dr. Madhu, the cardiologist; when he was examining Enasu in the casualty of hospital.

"I give deaf ear to laymen on medical matters." Dr. Madhu said in an expression less tone and ordered the warden to take the patient to ICCU at once. The attenders quickly pushed the stretcher towards the ICCU (IntensiveCoronary Care Unit).

Dr. Madhu and Thampy Swamy were neighbors in Santhinagar colony. They used to play badminton together occasionally. Dr. Madhu knew Thampy's character very well. A talkative and shrewd man. He talked about anything and everything under the sun, whether right or wrong that was his nature. He could not keep anything to himself, that was another bad side of him.

Though Dr. Madhu did not comment on his observations, Thampy concluded that Enasu was dead. His proactiveness made him think that he should be the first to inform the sad news to the world.

He passed messages to everyone know to him. "With great grief I inform you, our beloved chairman V.D Enasu passed away."

When Dr. Madhu declared that Enasu was out of danger all were relieved. But Thampy was embarrassed. He just slipped away from the crowd, not giving his face to them. He passed an another messege.

"A grave mistake by the hospital staff. Our chairman is out of danger. Please pray for his health. Regret for conveying wrong information given by the hospital without proper verification."

That was Thampy.A clever man who knew how to jump over a hurdle.

Later, Thampy was seen engaged in a discussion with Dr. Madhu.

"Enasu might have had problems with his heart muscles and might have ignored it for quite long." Dr. Madhu told to Thampy.

"Will he survive Dr. Madhu?" Thampy asked. His face became pale and throat was choked.

"God has to decide. But as a cardiologist I must say I have no hope. Please inform all his family members."

"I have already informed everyone. They are all on the way. His son Jobby, our executive director was in Madras yesterday. He has landed at Cochin airport about five minutes back, I received his call. He will be here at any moment. Second son Sabu is staying in Aluva. He is also on the way."

Joby, the second child of Enasu, about twenty-seven years of age, was a bit over sized, weighed about 98 kilograms was the executive director of PLPB Ltd. He was looking after the production and maintenance of the factory. He was a mechanical engineer and married to Gracy, a modest lady, a housewife and they had three children. They were staying at Vazhakala Bungalow along with his father and mother.

Third child Sabu, about twenty-six years of age was married to Mariam. They lived in a newly constructed bungalow at Aluva. They have a son. Sabu looks after the commercial part of the business, Marketing and export.

"What about his elder daughter Ancy? She is in Dubai now, isn't it? We were together in Alapuzha Medical College for MBBS. She opted post-graduation in ophthalmology and I went for cardiology. She is my age."

Thampy noticed Dr. Madu's face blush, when he referred about Ancy. "Both of you were in love, weren't you?" Thampy asked with a crooked smile.

"Hey, No... No... That was all just a gossip, not serious. How do you know that?"

Dr. Madhu wondered.

"I know everything in detail about the affairs of the chairman's family. He shares everything with me"

Thampy boasted and looked at Madhu with pride.

"Oh those are old stories, young age infatuation and nothing more. Let us not talk about it now."

"Her husband Dr. Jose is an ENT specialist. He is from Kottayam. A nice man. Both of them are jointly running a clinic in Dubai. The Sheiks are their patients and they are minting money I heard. They have two nice young deaughters." Thampy elaborated.

"Have you informed them?"

"Yes of course, Ancy has approached a travel agent to arrange fight tickets for today. She will be here by tomorrow early morning. I hope, Enasu sir will be alive till she reaches here."

"That is for sure" Dr. Madhu assured.

"Actually what is the problem? Is it a block?"

"Oh.... No....No, this is a heart rate falling issue. Normal resting heart beat rate is between sixty and hundred per minute. That is depending upon the person's physical condition and age. A healthy athletic heart beat can go lower up to fifty while resting. That's a good sign. While working the rate should not go below 60. Enasu's heart beat rate had gone down to twenty. That is near to the danger level. His heart muscles are very weak. I have tried my level best to increase the heart beat rate. But it is not going beyond forty. I have contacted Dr. Unnikrishnan of All India Institute of Medical Science for a consultation. He is an expert in this subject. I think he knows Enasu very well. When I mentioned the patient's name, I felt he got upset. That surprised me. He said he will come by the evening flight. But I don't think, it will help."

"Dr. Unnikrishnan" exclaimed Thampy, ... "Hey Doctor Madhu, .... You know who he is?

......Dr.Unnikrishnan is like his own son, more dear than Jobby and Sabu. He is my boss's best friend Rajasekharan's son. Rajasekharan was also a pilot in Indian Air Force. A group Captain. They were working together for so long."

"Oh....that's why doctor Unnikrishnan had expressed his concern on hearing the name of the patient. Anyway let him come."

"That's good news. I want to consult and discuss many things regarding the patient and his condition. Although he is of my same age, he is an expert and is senior to me by profession. Now he is a professor in AIIMSC."

Dr. Madhu seemed very happy to meet Dr. Unnikrishnan. Thampy saw Sabu's car entering the main gate of the hospital.

"Sabu sir is coming" Thampy said hastily.

As everyone anxiously watched them, Sabu came out of the car and hurriedly opened the rear door and helped his mother Jainamma to come out. Jobby's wife Gracy followed her.

Thampy ran towards them. He folded his hands and said to Jainamma. "Nothing to worry madam. Sir is perfectly alright."

He turned to Sabu and said "Good morning sir, it happened all of a sudden. Nobody expected it. He did not appear to be sick. He collapsed all of a sudden. But everything is under control now. I have taken care of everything."

They entered the veranda where Dr. Madhu was waiting for them. "Nothing to worry. Everything is under control." He told Jainamma.

Jainamma, even though aged fifty-eight, looked much younger. Her thick, grey curly hair, wrinklefree rosy cheeks and attractive eyes clearly proclaimed how good looking lady she was while young.

When Dr. Madhu held her arm and consoled her, her face suddenly became pale, eyes moistened and lips started to tremble.

"I have given him a sedative. Please don't disturb him now. You may see him from a distance"

Dr. Madu guided them to ICCU.

## 21. A foretell

Two hours passed since Enasu was admitted in the hospital. His heartbeat rate continued to be at twenty. He did not respond to medicines that were administered to him. However, Dr. Madhu did not declare that he was in a coma." He just said 'his condition is critical and under observation.'

"Dr. Unnikrishnan the renowned Cardiac specialist and professor of All India Institute of Medical Science, is called for specialized treatment and is on his way from Delhi by flight to attend the patient." The medical bulletin reported.

Enasu's children Joby and Sabu were seated in front of the ICCU ward. Joby was trying hard to suppress his emotions. But Sabu was intermittently sobbing very silently, covering his face with a handkerchief.

There was a special and extraordinary bonding between Enasu and his sons. Many people wondered and often asked him, how Enasu was able to build and sustain such a strong relation with his children.

"I live as per the doctrine of Christ." Was his answer.

"What is the doctrine of Christ?" That question would be asked suddenly. "Is it love?"

"Not love. It is the Righteousness". He would reply.

The factory manager Thampy Swamy was seated a little away from Joby and Sabu, but his attention was focused on them. He was ready to take up any orders that would be given to him.

All the factory workers of PLPB Ltd were gathered in the Courtyard of the hospital. They were anxiously waiting to know about the condition of their Chairman. Thampy instructed them to go back to the factory and continue their jobs, as that was the best thing they could do for their chairman. Yet many employees stayed back. The number of visitors from various sections of the community kept increasing.

A white ambassador car entered the main gate of the hospital and stopped near the entrance. A lofty aged man with grey crew-cut hair and thick grey mustache, wearing khaki pants and white shirt with double pockets came out from the driver's seat and walked swiftly to the ICCU ward.

That was Rajasekharan!

Five years ago, in 1995 Rajasekharan retired from Service on superannuation. He was fifty-five years old then. Since then, he was living alone in Achumana House, at Pallikara. His wife Rukmini died two years prior to his retirement. At that time, they were in Calcutta. She had uterus Cancer. It started with an abdominal pain and was wrongly diagnosed as Ulcer. Prolonged medication worsened the case. In order to remove the ulcer, she was operated upon. Doctors were shocked, when they saw that the cancer had already eaten away most of her internal organs. The dreadful disease was in its final stage.

Her cremation was done at Calcutta. Unnikrishnan came from London to attend the last rites. He was doing research in Alpha Medicare University on EMHS (ElectroMagnetic Heart Stimulating) Machine.

Enasu, Jainamma, Joby and Sabu were also present for the cremation but Ancy could not attend due to her exams. It was known that Unnikrishnan would be present, but Enasu deliberately avoided Ancy from accompanying them to Kolkata.

The ability to pinpoint and diagnose even a small illness is a divine gift. The new generation of doctors is yet to realize that truth.

As Rajasekharan entered the hospital, everyone who gathered there suspected that, he could be a Police top brass.

He went straight to the ICCU.

The head nurse rushed towards him to stop him. Before she could say anything Rajasekharan asked her "Where is Doctor Madhu.?"

Though he spoke softly, it reflected an authority. His face looked very serious. Dr. Madhu had seen him, rushed towards him with folded hands and greeted him with reveryence.

"Good morning Sir" He greeted, then told to the head nurse "you know who is this? This is Retired Group Captain Rajasekharan, father of Dr. Unnikrishnan of AIIMS, for whom we are all waiting."

The head nurse suddenly bowed her head and greeted Rajasekharan deep respect.

"How is Enasu?" Rajasekharan asked.

Dr. Madhu explained to him the condition of the patient, while walking towards Enasu's bed.

"Dr. Unnikrishnan is expected here by four in the evening." Madhu said. "Yes I know. He phoned me from the airport."

Enasu was lying between two drip stands, tubes were connected to his wrist veins of both the arms. Oxygen mask was attached to help him breath, he was unconscious. His heartbeat was visible on the screen of Cardiac monitor. Two nurses were closely attending to him.

Rajasekharan's eyes became moistened. He was reminded of the hospitalization of his friend nineteen years ago, when his knee was smashed in aircraft explosion due to missile attack by Pakistan army.

There he was lying in the same posture, unconscious. At that time, he was afraid of his leg being amputated. But God saved him. Even with an artificial knee he could walk. But now his life itself is in danger.

A steel chair was brought for Rajasekharan. He pulled out a handkerchief from his pocket and wiped out his tears. He thought of a telephonic conversation he had with Enasu some days back. It was an unusual talk and his tone was also unusal. Rajasekharan did not like it.

Had he fallen prey to his own calamitous foreboding? Rajasekharan thought to himself.

"Hey Raja, I have a feeling that my time is up." He had said over the phone.

"For what?" Rajasekharan asked.

"For my last journey."

"To where?"

"From where I had come from."

Rajasekharan did not like his talk. His tone and topic irritated him.

"Hey, you can't go back to your mother's womb again man." He said.

"Only the foetus come out from the womb. The life in it, is coming from its origin."

"Oh, the same theory of yours! To hell with you. The life after death will join back with its origin, the power of nature, the originator of life, is that what you mean? How many times you have told me the same stuff. What is the relevance?"

"It is relevant. Raja. It is the truth"

"What?"

"My time has come; I have that feeling."

"You mean to say you are going to die?" Rajasekharan laughed, but a pain pinched in his heart.

"Man you are only sixty now. The average life of man is seventy - seventy-five. Many more years to go for both of us."

"No Raja. I am sure, my time has come. I have a strong instinct. I can hear my death bells ring." Enasu said in a serious tone.

Rajasekharan got upset, but told him in an annoyed tone. "Then you go to the church and make your last confessions with your priest and ask him for the last sacraments. So that you need not trouble him when you die. If possible, buy a coffin and start sleeping in it."

"Rajan, you know that I don't believe in rituals. They are all bloody bogus and superstitions."

"Why are you telling me all these bullshit now?" Rajasekharan asked in an annoyed manner.

"I am not cutting jokes Raja. I am serious.... There is something happening in me."

"What?" Rajasekharan felt wired. "I feel that my heart beat is stopping now and then for a short while. A sort of missing. I am getting that feeling intermittently."

"Hey man. Why don't you go to some doctor and consult? Unni is expected by next week. You go to that Medical College. Dr. Madhu is good. I know him. Whenever Unni comes here, Madhu used to call him for some discussion."

"Yes? I think will go to him."

"You want me to come with you. I am free. You just tell me...... your time, I will be there."

"Oh. Don't bother. I will take care of myself."

He might have not gone to the doctor, Rajasekharan thought.

Rajasekharan got up from the chair, had a close look on Enasu's face again and walked out of ICCU ward.

Joby and Sabu were waiting for him at the door itself. He embraced Sabu, gave a hug to Joby and three of them walked towards bystander's room where Jainamma was waiting.

## 22. Electro magnetic cardiac stimulator

"Hospitals are keeping dead bodies in ventilators"

That was the headline on that day's evening newspaper 'Critics'. Even after the death of patients, hospitals continue to keep the dead body under ventilator for plundering, the paper accused.

Though the paper 'Critics' was known as a "Gossip Spreader" there were certain facts and hidden truths in their statements always. The 'Critics' had wide acceptance in the town. The paper had a circulation of about one hundred thousand copies in the city. The civil authorities and police disliked it, as they were referred very frequently in the paper.

The 'Critics' had expressed their concern over the condition of the renowned industrialist, writer, and theosophist Enasu. His ailment could not be used for plundering by the hospitals. The report caused more people to pour into the hospital to know about his condition.

By evening Dr. Unnikrishnan reached the hospital. There were two junior doctors at the airport to receive him.

All gathered at hospital recognized Dr. Unnikrishnan, the most renowned cardiologist of All India Institute of Medical Sciences, Delhi, whose photos appear very often in newspapers. He looked lean and tall with trimmed beard and had sharp looking eyes. There was a "chandana Kuri" (a mark worn on forehead) on his forehead with Sandal paste which denoted his faith in Hindu religion. He wore a "Rudraksha Mala" around his neck. He wore black pants and saffron coloured 'Juba Shirt' (lengthy shirt without color) and its sleeves were rolled up to his elbow.

Joby and Sabu had seen him coming out of the car, and they were very happy. Both of them ran to him. It was a much unexpected reunion of brothers. Three of them embraced each other and talked for some time.

In the past two years, Unnikrishnan was in London doing research on a certain Cardiographic machine, at "Alpha Cross hospital and Research Foundation" widely known as ACHRF London, as a delegate from All India Institute of Medical Sciences known as AIIMS Delhi.

Joby and Sabu could not contact Unnikrishnan as, they never knew that Unnikrishnan was back in Delhi.

"It is wonderful that you have come" Joby Said.

"I had talked to Dad a month ago over the phone from London regarding an issue. Our property at Pallikara is under a case now. Apparently, they claim that Acha is having three other siblings. They are said to be illegal children of my Grandfather Parameswarn Nair. They have a claim on our property. Acha had filed a counter suit in the court against their claim. Related to that issue I had a talk with Dad. He told me that there is nothing to be worried about. At that time, he told me he had some chest pain. I advised him to go to Dr. Madhu and consult him."

"I did not know all this. Dad never told me." Joby lamented

"It's ok, you know our Dad. He never reveals his problems, it's not anyone's fault."

"Dr. Madhu had called me. Anyway, let me have a look. Don't worry" Unnikrishnan Said.

Dr. Madhu ran to them and greeted Unnikrishnan with due reverence. Unnikrishnan was his professor during his post graduation.

"I was not aware sir, that you had connection with Enasu Sir." Dr. Madhu said.

"We are one family. I address your patient as Dad.... Yes... He is my Dad."

Dr. Madhu directed Dr. Unnikrishnan to ICCU.

It was a thirty bed ICCU ward, with all modern facilities. Only ten beds were occupied. Enasu's bed was on a corner. Two junior doctors and three nurses were near Enasu's bed. All of them greeted Dr. Unnikrishnan with deep respect and reverence.

They all considered it as a golden opportunity to be with Dr. Unnikrishnan, the famous cardiologist who received gold Medal from President of India for his Cardiological Research and findings.

Unnikrishnan stood at the foot of Enasu's bed. He looked at the patient with an inquisitive eye. Slowly his eyes became narrowed and a deep reverence reflected on his face. His eyes became moistened. He extended his hands and gripped Enasu's feet. He held them for some time. Then withdrew and touched his own forehead with a silent murmur in his lips. That was the Hindu traditional custom for expressing respect to the parents.

'Dr. Madhu and other doctors were astonished by his actions. Unnikrishnan might have received a lot of help from the rich man, they thought.

Unnikrishnan instructed Dr. Madhu to make arrangements to offload the equipment from the car boot, which he had brought along with him from Delhi.

There were two boxes and a bundle of cables in the car. Two attenders brought the heavy boxes to Enasu's bed with a lot of effort.

Unnikrishnan examined Enasu with his stethoscope and closely watched the heart beat monitor. X -ray and ECG chart were also verified.

He asked one of the junior doctors to open the boxes. One box was a monitor with control panel. The big box was a power unit and magnetic wave radiator with Klystron valve. Cable rolls were wound and connected to a Power plug on the wall having 230 Volts. Other four cables, were for inter connection between both the boxes. Six small cables were connected to Enasu's nerve centers with suction clips as ECG connectors. He took two thin cables having one end with clip connectors and other end, with long sharp steel needles of seven inches' length, and thickness of one millimeter. The needle ends were very sharp like pins. Clip connectors were connected to a monitor.

When all the medicos and nurses were eagerly looking upon, he switched on the main power unit. A hissing sound was heard and so many neon lights were glowed. The fluorescent screen on the monitor glowed like an oscilloscope. Some numbers and letters appeared on the screen along with live reflection of the throbbing heart of the patient. A digital meter indicated the pulse rate of the patient.

He held the needle in both his hands, he turned his face to the onlookers.

The doctors and nurses were watching his gestures with mixed feeling of anxiety and inquisitiveness. Their facial expression seemed as if, they were watching a horror movie. "Now, look all of you." Unnikrishnan started to talk to them like a professor.

"This equipment is the latest invention in the medical science of cardiology. This equipment is known as EMC stimulator, Electromagnetic Cardiac stimulator. It's not introduced for treatment so far. There are only six equipment of this kind, made so far. And I am one of the six researchers equipped with it. With this equipment a new method of treatment would be introduced to stimulate weak muscles of heart.

This equipment will produce ultra high frequency of electro magnetic waves. When such waves with high amplitude are made to pass through the heart through these sharp needles, the weak muscles would get stimulated... That is the theory... Now look,"

Unnikrishnan turned to the patient. By looking at the monitor, where the throbbing heart was projected alive, he pierced both the sharp long needles directly to the heart of the patient. Blood appeared at the pierced point of the needles. He put cotton gauze at the pierced point to block the blood.

Another switch was put on. The machine started humming. Electromagnetic waves started passing through the weak muscles of the patient. The heart started to vibrate and it could be seen on the monitor. There was a flickering of pulse on the heart pulse indicator. Slowly the level of heart beat started to increase. Within two minutes, the pulse rate increased to eighty-five, and became steady.

Enasu opened his eyes.

## 23. Peeling a scab

The next day before dawn Enasu's eldest daughter Dr. Ancy about 28 years of age, with her husband Dr. Jose, and their two young daughters Julie and Laly landed at Cochin Airport. The Dubai flight was delayed by half an hour. Sabu was there at the airport to receive them.

It was drizzling then. Julie and Laly enjoyed the rain. They felt ecstatic when tiny droplets of rain fell on them like pearls from the sky. It was a heavenly feeling for them.

Ancy was very upset and worried about her father's ailment. Thampy's phone call was very alarming. She was afraid that she would not see her Dad alive. Throughout the flight she was praying rosary.

Ancy embraced her younger brother Sabu and sobbed loudly, ignoring it was a public place and people were watching them.

"Hey, what is this Ancy, I don't understand why you are crying now. It's alright. Dad has fully recovered. He will come out of ICCU by noon. There is no need to cry now. "Sabu consoled his sister in an annoyed tone.

Even otherwise, crying on any silly matter was her habit disorder from childhood. She was mocked by everybody at home "weeping doll'.

From airport, Sabu drove them directly to the hospital. Thampy swamy was waiting for them. He guided them to the bystander's room in the new block of the hospital where Jainamma and other family members were camping in prayers.

It was very early in the morning. Jainamma was sitting on her bed and praying rosary alone in silence. Gracy, wife of Joby, Mariam wife of Sabu and their three children were sleeping on mats on the floor.

It was a part of routine for Jainamma to get up at five in the morning and pray rosary, though Enasu was not in acceptance of intercessory prayers. His theory on God and mode of prayer were different, which was not acceptable to Jainamma. Other than this theological indifference Enasu and Jainamma never had any difference of opinion in any matters.

"I am not interested in your big theory of omnipotent God, without name and figure. I believe in Jesus Christ as my God and it is the same that your omnipotent substance. I call that Omnipotent as Christ and you call it as the spirit of nature. Both are the same. Why don't you understand this silly logic?" Jainamma had argued once.

On that very morning Jainamma prayed, "Oh…. My Ensasu's omnipotent spirit, my Jesus Christ, thank you for saving my husband's life by sending Unni in time with his magic machine."

The door was pushed open and Ancy busted in. She embraced her mother and sobbed. Jainamma pushed her away and said irritably. "There is nothing to cry now. We must rejoice and say thanks to God for saving your Dad's life. God appeared personally in the form of our Unni and saved his life."

"Unni?" Ancy's face flushed up with surprise "Is Unni here? I was told, he was in London."

"If my Unni did not reach here on time, your Dad would not have survived. He saved your Dad. It was lucky for us that he had returned from England just a few days back." Jainamma Said.

"It was a resurrection indeed." Thampy who was standing at the door watching them added, "Dr. Madhu the Chief Cardiologist here had almost lost hope on your dad's life. In fact, he had never expected your dad would recover at all. Dr. Unnikrishnan had brought a magical equipment with him. With that machine he regularized your father's heartbeat and saved his life. He was half dead, no he was almost dead when we brought him here. God is great.

Dr. Unnikrishnan is brilliant. "What magical equipment are you talking about? Do you know its name?" Ancy asked.

"No, Ancy madam. Even Dr. Madhu has never heard of such a machine. It is a new invention."

"I am a doctor; I've never heard of such a machine." Ancy's voice was furious.

"Hey Ancy, don't argue on that issue with Thampy. You ask Unni. He is sitting just by the side of dad's bed in ICCU. He has not taken any food nor a cup of tea ever since he came yesterday evening" Sabu said.

"Unni is my son, though not from my womb." Jainamma said with lot of affection in her voice.

"I want to see my dad." Ancy said in hurry.

"I suggest not to disturb him now. He might be sleeping. He will be brought to room within a few hours. It is better, if you wait for some time." Sabu suggested.

"No. I want to see him now." Ancy's voice was adamant." Where is the ICCU...?"

" At the far end of the corridor...... Turn left, then go straight."

"I will show you. Please come with me Madam." Thampy, volunteered and both left the room.

When Ancy left the room with Thampy Dr. Jose, husband of Ancy, approached his mother - In law and greeted her with folded hands and kissed her forehead with lot of reverence. His two children, Julie and Laly four and six years of age had already sat on both the sides of their grandmother, their hands tightly rounded on her waist. Jainamma caressed the heads of her young grandchildren with both hands and kissed their cheeks.

"I am not going to ICCU now, I will meet dad when he is shifted to the room." Dr. Jose sat on chair.

Ancy entered the ICCU ward very cautiously.

"Are you Dr. Ancy? Daughter of Enasu Sir?" Duty nurse asked.

Ancy being an ophthalmologist was not familiar with ICCU wards. In fact, she was afraid to enter an ICCU. She had a feeling that ICCU's are the houses of death houses.

Though there were thirty-six beds in that ICCU, only ten were occupied. All the occupied beds were in one side, and Enasu's bed was in the corner of the other side. The ward seemed to be empty. There only two small, night lamps were glowing and the light was very dim.

The snoring grunts of the patients were heard loudly. The "Peep - Peep' sounds of the pulse oxinators fitted over their heads were also heard, in different tones, like background music of a horror cinema.

Enasu was lying between two drip stands on a high raised slanted bed. Dr. Unnikrishnan was sitting on a chair by the side of the bed. The EMCS equipment detached from Enasu's body was kept by the side. Its cables were rolled and kept over the equipment, ready to use again if necessary. A small table with a table lamp was provided for Unnikrishnan, and he was writing something on a clip pad under the focused light of the table lamp.

She was about to meet Unnikrishnan after Nine years. She noticed a lot of changes in him. He looked very aged and very serious.

Ancy stood looking at her father for sometime. She turned to Unnikrishnan with a sigh. Unnikrishnan had seen Ancy, but did not look up and continued his writing. Ancy understood that she was ignored.

"Unni, you may please go and take rest. I will sit here." She said to Unnikrishnan in a whispering voice.

"What is the use of you here? I am monitoring his pulse rate minute by minute, looking for variation if any." He said with an authority in his voice. That irritated Ancy. "Unni, I am also a doctor. I also know, how to check the pulse rate of a patient."

"This is a cardiac case madam, not an eyesore. An ophthalmologist will never be able to guess what the consequence would be of the variation in amplitude or duration of the heartbeat of a cardiac patient."

"Is it that magic equipment they are all talking about?" Ancy asked pointing at the cardiac instrument.

"It is not a magic equipment. It is known as EMCS, electromagnetic cardiac stimulator. Newly developed but not yet approved by the medical Council. It is used to stimulate the heart muscles by electromagnetic waves."

Then he explained how the machine works. Ancy listened to his lecture with interest.

"Are you sure the patient won't get electric shock when an electromagnetic wave is directly passed through the heart?" She asked like a student.

"You fool. Don't you know, the EM wave is not electric? First you learn what EM Wave is".

Unnikrishnan was annoyed by her question, but Ancy enjoyed irritating him, just like in their childhood.

But Unni suddenly said in regret. : "I am sorry."

"What for Unni?"

"I should have not talked to you like that."

"You have the right Unni."

"Stop it…... Stop it." He said in an arrogant manner.

"Still you are annoyed on me Unni?" Tears rolled down her cheeks.

Unnikrishnan looked down and was silent.

"Unni, that is over and past. Now eight years have gone by. Still you could not forget that unfortunate incident Unni?" Unnikrishnan did not answer.

"Still you keep a grudge on me…. It was all my mistake."

"Hey no... Not at all…. It was my mistake."

"Can't you stop this penance.... For heaven sake?"

"Penance? What do you mean by that?"

"Why are you living like a monk? You are a respectful and well known cardiologist now. Your beard, saffron shirt, rudraksha necklace and sandal paste on your forehead etc are not suitable for a doctor.... This comic dress is really absurd." She said in annoyed tone, but with love.

"You better mind your own business." Unnikrishnan's voice was harsh.

"Still you hate me. ...?" She sobbed and turned back to go away.

"Ancy......" Enasu's voice was heard loudly and very clearly. Ancy was shocked, and she turned back.

Unnikrishnan also was shocked and looked at his father with widened eyes. He looked at the pulse monitor, and found Enasu's heart beat level had reached to normal. Very normal. He checked his chest with Stethoscope, and found it to be perfect.

"My God, Dad, you are back...Back to normal." Unnikrishnan exclaimed. Ancy ran to her father and sat by the side of Enasu, and held his face with both the hands and cried, "Dad.........Dad." She kissed both his checks. Duty nurses and doctors watched what was happening from a distance. They were reluctant to go closer as Unnikrishnan was examining the patient.

"Unni! my son......!" Enasu said in a loud voice.

That voice contained mixed feelings of happiness, love and affection.

He held Unnikrishnan's hand and said, "Unni, I was listening to your conversations. It is too bad to peel out the scab of a healing wound. The scab has to be shed on its own. Peeling out the scab means you are refreshing the wound and inflicting more pain. That is not good at all. Do you understand what I mean?

"Yes Dad!"

"She is your sister…. Treat her accordingly…. With love and care."

"Yes dad!"

"Ancy... "He called. "Daughter, he is your own brother by all means."

"Yes Dad."

But she did not understand the hidden meaning of "By all means."

## 24. Trima hospital

Enasu was hospitalized only for four days. His heart rate became normal and he seemed to be very active and cheerful as before.

The very next day of his discharge from hospital, he resumed his official duty. The entire factory workers and staff gathered at the factory gate to give him a warm welcome. They were all delighted to see their boss back into office.

Ancy and her family returned to Dubai the very next day. Enasu was discharged from hospital. Joby and Sabu continued to engage in factory affairs, as usual.

Sabu was thrilled when he received a bulk export order for fresh flowers. The order was from the world renowned flower merchant "Inter Flora" Singapore. Sabu had started the horticulture as a hobby but it turned out to be very profitable business. He was procured fresh flowers from Bangalore and Ooty, and exported them, well packed in printed cartons.

Sabu had developed a particular type of fresh flower preservative to spray on fresh flowers. Once sprayed, the life of the flowers would last long. It was an organic lacquer, transparent in nature and odorless. It prevents the evaporation of water content from the petals of flowers and thus the freshness would be maintained, without withering and color fading. However, its fragrance would be lost after a few days of its application, but that could be compensated by spraying perfumes.

"It is a great achievement. Do not reveal the basis of chemical combination and manufacturing process to anyone" Enasu advised Sabu.

He did not reveal it to anyone. Later he made millions of dollars by selling the technology to a Japanese Company, "Yoho Horo."

Unnikrishnan postponed his return journey to Delhi. He was planning to establish a 'Super specialty heart hospital' in Cochin. The All India Institute of

Medical Sciences had given their consent to establish such a hospital in Kerala under their affiliation.

The name of the project was "Trima Medicare Hospital" and the project cost was fifteen crores (One hundred and fifty million rupees). The State Bank of India, New Delhi had given him a Principle approval for term loan of one hundred million rupees against collateral security of ten acres of land and Achumana house at Pallikara, for which Rajasekharan had to sign as guarantor.

But all the plans went astray. Three claimants said to be the Co- brothers of Rajasekharan, namely Ravi, Chandran and Gopi from North Parur filed a claim on Anchumana house and Pallikara property.

They said that, the Co–brothers were the illicit sons of Rajasekharan's father Parameswaran Nair, while he was in his deathbed had accepted the three of them as his own sons born to his illicit wife Radha.

As per law, licit or illicit children are equally entitled for the share of their father's ancestral property. The claim by the illicit sons of Rajasekharan's father, was accepted by the court and a verdict was passed in their favour. As per the order three fourth of property would be given to the so called Co -brothers.

Thus, Rajasekharan's ownership on the property was limited to two and a half acres, which was not sufficient for the bank to sanction the loan for THMC hospital. Rajasekharan and Unnikrishnan, became very upset and desperate.

"District court is not the final authority. There is a high court and also a Supreme Court. We will contest the verdict in high Court. "Enasu consoled them.

The company lawyer Nambiar was called immediately to the Cabin and was introduced to Rajasekharan and Unnikrishnan.

"I've read a lot about you in newspapers doctor Unnikrishnan. We are proud of you and happy to see you" Nambiar complimented.

Enasu handed over a copy of the court order to him and said. "We must get a favourable order from High court. And that should be done urgently."

"Sir, this is a civil case. It will take at least six months for the case to be called for hearing."

"Make it criminal then? "

"No. I will make it as an urgent case to be heard immediately. But it will be expensive."

"Forget about the money man."

"Then it is done."

"Nambiar, please check up the scheduled price of land in Pallikkara. In case compensation is suggested, let it be in the scheduled price. Understand?" Enasu gave him a caution.

The case was called within ten days. That was a record time in the history of high court. But the verdict was in favour of the illicit children of Parameswaran Nair. High court upheld the lower court judgment. However, there was a clause included in the order. "The illicit children could be paid their share value in cash as per the scheduled rate of land stipulated by the government and published in "Government gazette."

Rajasekharan and Unnikrishnan became disheartened when they read the verdict. But Enasu laughed loudly.

"What is there to laugh?" Rajasekharan asked arrogantly.

"What do you think of our Advocate Nambiar, he made the judge to write the verdict in our favour, but maintained the righteousness also."

"I did not get it." Rajasekharan was puzzled.

"Use your brain and open your eyes man. Read the second part of the verdict. Raja you can hold the right of the entire property by paying them their share value as cash"

"But it will be a lot of money. The value of one cent would be three to four lakhs."

"You are talking about the local market value. But court is ordering us to pay at the scheduled rate declared by the state Government. The schedule was fixed ten years back and the scheduled rate at Pallikara area is just three hundred rupees per cent. They are entitled for their share of seven and half acres. The total cost of their shares as per the scheduled rate would be seven hundred and fifty multiplied by three hundred and it is two lakhs twenty-five thousand only understand?"

Rajasekharan and Unnikrishnan became wonder stuck. Rajasekharan looked at Enasu with tears in his eyes and Unnikrishnan looked at him with a lot of pride.

"By the way, Unni, what is THMC Hospital? What does THMC stand for?" Enasu asked.

"That is Trima Heart Medi Care Hospital."

"What is this Trima?"

Unnikrishnan was silent for some time then said." Trima means three mothers. One to deliver. One to feed and one to nurture."

Unnikirshnan's eyes were reflected with mixed feelings of joy, gratification and sadness. Slowly, his eyes became moistened.

"Hey Unni, my son. You are great and I am very grateful. God will bless you"

"Your blessings are the Gods blessings for me." He said.

"May I ask you one thing Unni? Enasu asked. Why do you want a loan from bank for this beautiful project? There is no hospital in Cochin, exclusively for heart ailments. If we establish such a hospital, it will be a blessing to this state."

"But it is a very costly project Dad."

"OK... that's Ok. You have projected fifteen crores for this project. I have gone through your project report. You have not considered the working capital in the project. If you consider working capital about three crores, the total cost would be eighteen crores. That is not a large issue. We can raise that much money without a bank loan. The bank interest will eat away the profit. Sometimes it will affect the capital also. We will go for a public issue."

Unnikrishnan looked at Enasu with confusion. "I don't know anything about business Dad." He said.

"OK. Then I will tell you what has to be done."

He picked up the intercom and asked his PA to come in.

"Raju. Please call Joby and Sabu and ask them to come immediately. Call, our Chartered Accountant George, Advocate Nambiar and Finance Manager Saly and GM to be present in our conference room by eleven. We will come there after tea." It was an order by the Chairman.

By eleven sharp all were seated in the conference room. Enasu addressed the meeting. Except Joby and Sabu all were ready to take notes in their diaries. That was the usual practice.

"We are going to establish a hospital project as a sister concern of our company. It will be a private limited company. It will be a heart specialty hospital and first of its kind in Kerala. The hospital will be affiliated to AIIMS Delhi. That is equivalent to having a branch of AIIMS in Cochin. The location will be at Pallikkara, where we are having ten acres of free hold land. Present market value of the land is to be capitalized.........

"This hospital will be promoted by our company and it will be a private limited company and the shares will be issued by private placement. Shares will be issued to a few selected hospitals who would like to associate with our heart specialty hospital. I am sure that all the hospitals in Kerala would be interested to join us as the hospital is headed by Dr. Unnikrishan of AIIMS and affiliated to AIIMS. Each participant hospital would invest one crore rupees as shares towards equity participation....

"Now regarding Article of Association and Memorandum. I will be the Chairman of the new company and all directors of our company will be directors of this new company. Rajasekharan and Unnikrishnan will be additional shareholders. Rajasekharan will be The Vice Chairman and Dr. Unnikrishnan will be The Permanent Managing Director of the Company. A detailed profile would be made by George our CA.

"We will ask the interested hospitals for an advance remittance of fifty percent, that is, fifty lakhs rupees as call money, at the time of submitting their share application and balance remittance after the approval of allotment of shares by the Board. Fifty percent of the total project cost would be invested by our company PLPB Ltd...."

Enasu was dictating the plans, as if it was predetermined. His narration continued, and it was like a Military General giving orders.

"The name of the company is THMC hospital, that is, Trima Heart Speciality Medicare hospital, Pallikkara, Cochin."

Enasu concluded the discussion. It was not a meeting but an announcement of decisions to be implemented without any question being asked.

Rajasekharan said in his mind. "He is still a Daredevil"

## 25. Tragic end of Raphel

The first person, who visited Enasu after resuming his office was Fr. Robin Padipura, the very aged priest, who was running, St. Marys Old Age Home, in Kottackal house at Nellikunnu near Kothamangalam.

Enasu got up from his seat, greeted the aged priest with due reverence, and offered him a seat in front of him.

Enasu was meeting Fr. Robin after a period of ten years. They haven't seen each other since his father-in- law Raphel's funeral in 1990. At that time Fr. Robin had put up a request to allow him to continue the functioning of the old age home in Kottackal house, in which he and his aged father was living. Fr. Robin was released from Parish duties and permission was granted by bishop for his stay in old age home along with his father and other inmates and he was instructed to offer the Mass at Nellikunnu church daily.

Raphel wanted to construct a separate house in the enclosures and live independently. But he was very depressed and mentally ill. He became mentally sick due to excessive suppression of tension and mental worries. The sickness was developed from the sadness hidden in the subconscious mind caused due to the tragic death of his dear daughter Elamma.

The mental disorder developed in him gradually and he became silent and aloof. He had lost interest in everything. He was very broody and it became necessary to compel him even for his wash and bath.

On hearing the sad news, Enasu and Jainamma rushed to Kottackal house. They wanted to take Raphel to Delhi along with them to treat him in Air Force hospital. But Raphel denied categorically. When he was compelled, he became more adamant and ferocious. He did not show any intimacy to Enasu and expressed arrogance on him. That hurt Enasu very badly.

Fr. Robin consoled him. "Don't worry son. I will take care of your father. The old age home is meant to take care of such parents.

Thus, Kottackal Raphel, the owner of the house became an inmate of the old age home.

It was the daily routines of Raphel to go to church to attend the Mass in the morning and then he would go to the cemetery alone and sit on the tomb of Elamma in which his wife Saramma also was buried earlier.

It was a regular, everyday sight for the natives to see the old man Raphel sitting at the tomb in cemetery alone.

One day the sexton of the church saw that old man Raphel was lying on the marble slab of the tomb. Sexton ran to him and checked. Raphel was dead by then.

Jainamma became hysterical at the time of funeral of her father. She fell unconscious, when the body was buried. All the children of Enasu, Rajasekharan and Rukmini attended the funeral.

"Now Raphel is gone and Jainamma is the owner of the house, in which me, my ailing father and seven aged inmates are living. Will you allow us to continue the functioning of our old age home in your house at Kottackal?" Fr. Robin asked Enasu, after the funeral when all were about to leave.

"By all means father. You can continue to stay here along with your inmates. In the meantime, please look after our property in the enclosure. There are fourteen acres of land with rubber and coconut trees. They are not looked after well. Please do something to maintain it. You may take all the yields from the enclosure for your expenditure." Enasu said.

"It is very kind of you Enasu. May God bless you! Truly speaking, we were already living with the yields from the property. It was Raphel's kindness and generosity. He was more than a brother to me."

Ten years passed. Enasu never got a chance to visit Kottackal house or to meet Fr. Robin.

The same father Robin was in front of him in his cabin. He looked very aged and tired.

"I read in the paper about your ailment, and hospitalization. I could not come and meet you. I was also in hospital." Fr. Robin said.

"What happened to you Father? Why were you hospitalized?"

"I have memberships in so many clubs now. Diabetics club, Pressure club, Cholesterol club etc. Now they say my kidney is also gone....

My father is no more. He died six years ago but still I am not free since, I have four helpless old people in my old age home. Now I am also sick. I am not in a position to look after myself, then how would I take care of the inmates? I requested our bishop to take care of those four old souls and give me refuge in the priest's retirement house. He agreed to do so, but in return he asked me to find out whether there is any possibility of getting your house and enclosure, as donation to the diocese. He has plans to build a good orphanage there, if he gets that house and enclosure"

"Does he realize what he is asking?" Enasu said, very irritated. "The political leaders and church authorities would never have any delicacy or decency in asking for donations." Enasu said.

"Our procurator's brain is behind it. Bishop is an innocent soul."

"All are the same. There are very few clergymen like you living for others. Most of the new generation priests are after fame and money. What to do? You need not worry about the inmates of Kottackal house. I will shift them to another old age home in Ernakulam. You may please hand over the keys of the house to our manager, who will come there to transfer the aged people. And you may go and take rest in your priest's house, father."

"Very kind of you Enasu.... God will bless you."

Fr. Robin came out of Enasu's cabin satisfied with his decision.

## 26. Heavenly Intercessor

Rajasekharan along with Unnikrishnan, paid a visit to Enasu in his office. Both of them looked very tensed.

The report on, starting a heart specialty hospital with affiliation to AIIMS Delhi, was welcomed by all the hospital groups in Kerala.

The detailed brochure of THMC hospital was well appreciated by all cardiologists. Some commented in newspapers that, "It is the need of the time".

Fifty hospitals from different parts of Kerala confirmed their interest in the equity participation of the project. Applications with cheques for fifty lakh rupees being advance remittance towards equity participation were received from them. It was quite unexpected.

"We don't want any extra fund other than the fund required for the implementation of the project". Enasu said categorically.

"Total project cost as per the revised project study by experts is twenty crores. Fifty-one percentage would be invested by our company PLPB Limited. That is eleven crores. Balance requirement is only nine crores.

We will select nine Mission Hospitals to associate with us. How many Mission hospitals have applied?" Enasu asked to Finance Manager, Saly.

"Nineteen Sir"

"Select Nine out of them. There are many money making hospitals working in the name of mission hospital, in Kerala. We will select only the real service oriented mission hospitals."

"Yes Sir."

"Please return all other applications along with their cheques. Do not forget to write them our sincere thanks for their interest and good faith in our new endeavor."

Everything was set to start the construction work of THMC hospital building complex. Six bulldozers were working day and night for four days for the site development. Cutting down all the yielding nutmeg trees planted and grown by Rajasekharan was heartbreaking for him. All the required licenses and permits were also received.

Dr. Unnikrishnan approached Enasu with a peculiar request.

"Dad, I want to visit my mom's tomb."

Enasu looked at him very surprisingly.

"Unni, don't you know, she was cremated in Calcutta? It was done in electric crematorium. There won't be any tomb or monument there. Details will be recorded in their register" Enasu said.

"Not my Amma, Dad! I mean my mom who gave birth to me, Elamma."

Enasu's face fell. A shock like a lightning pierced through his heart. His heart wriggled with pain. He became upset, but pretended to be normal.

"I don't know, if any tomb is left over there in that cemetery". Enasu had difficulty to say even that much. His throat was choked.

"I understand that my mom was buried in the family tomb of Kottackal at Kothamangalam church cemetery, where my grandfather Raphel was also buried". Unnikrishnan said.

"Who told you all these?"

"My mummy. She told me that her sister Elamma died of cancer. Let it be like that."

Enasu did not ask him why they had a conversation about Elamma.

"Yes... yes... now I remember. There was a family tomb and she was buried in there." Enasu managed to say that much.

Immediately they proceeded to Kothamangalam in Enasu's Benz Car. Enasu avoided taking his personal chauffeur Anil to Kothamangalam.

Unnikrishnan drove the car. It was a one-hour drive. Throughout the journey both of them were silent. They were plunged into their own different thoughts. Enasu was letting out deep sighs of despair intermittently as if he was desperate.

The cemetery was full of bush and high grasses. There were hundreds of graves with mud heaps planted with wooden crosses over them. Very few tombs were seen.

They found out the "Kottakal family tomb". It was constructed with white marble. The entire tomb was covered with grass creepers with lot of small white flowers on them. Unnikrishnan removed the grass creepers from the top of white marble slab. The engraved letters on the slab were visible.

Three people were buried in that tomb. The first name was Saramma, wife of Raphel Kottackal. She died in 1952. The second was Elamma. Born in 1950 died 3rd August 1972. The third was Raphel Kottakkal died in 1990. He was 65 years of age.

Unnikrishnan walked quickly to the car, brought a bouquet and placed it on the top of the tomb. He stood silently for some time, with closed eyes and folded hands.

Enasu stood just behind Unnikrishnan watching, his movements and gestures. His mind was trembling violently with mixed emotions.

He tried hard to be non-expressive. But he started sweating. He tried hard to hold his tears. He bit his lips tightly to stop it from shivering.

The pain inflicted in his chest, when Unnikrishnan had expressed his desire to visit Elamma's tomb continued to subsist. He felt tired, and wanted to sit somewhere.

He walked back to his car, opened the front left door ajar and sat on the seat, he felt weak. He picked up the water bottle kept by the side of the driver's seat and drank in big gulps till the bottle became empty.

Unnikrishnan plucked a fist full of flower from the grass creepers of the tomb.

"Dad I want these flowers to be laid along with the foundation stone of our hospital building." He requested Enasu.

Enasu nodded as an approval. He was not in a position to talk anything at that time. He was trying to suppress a sob.

The foundation stone laying ceremony was performed without any publicity. The stone was laid by Jainamma. When she was given a fistful of the withered small flowers to put them on top of the foundation stone, she asked. "Where are these withered flowers from? Is it from a holy place?"

"These are blessed flowers Mummy" Unnikrishnan said.

"By whom?" Jainamma asked.

Unnikrishnan was silent for some time. Then said "By my God"

"You should have brought our Parish priest to bless the foundation stone." Jainamma complained to Enasu.

"Blessing has to come from God. Not from a priest"

Enasu's reply was not liked by his wife.

"Priests represent God"

"Who taught you this blunder? Priests represent the church. God does not have any representatives or agents in the world. He would directly involve in all deeds of all living souls, regardless of their size or shape." It was a declaration of his faith.

Jainamma kept mum. She knew, Enasu was a blind believer of omnipotent God and not a God defined by religion.

The construction work of the hospital building started on the same day in full speed. One hundred people were working at the site.

Next day morning, a loud cry was heard from Enasu's bedroom. It was Jainamma. Her shrill voice was heard up to the outhouse of the Vazhakala Bungalow. All at home and the people working around the house ran to the bed room very frantically.

Enasu was lying on his bed covered with a bed sheet, as if he was sleeping very comfortably.

He used to get up at six in the morning daily. That day he had not come out of his bedroom even after seven thirty. When Jainamma came back from the church at seven thirty, she found her husband still in bed, which was very unusual. She shook him by his shoulder to wake him up. When there was no movement she checked. The body was very stiff and cold.... She cried aloud.

The postmortem report stated that Enasu died of cardiac arrest and that it happened before midnight.

It was a very silent death. Even Jainamma who was lying beside never knew.

The natives of Kakanadukara believed that it is a miracle that the fresh flowers used to decorate the tomb of Enasu did not wither away or become discoloured even after seven days! The tomb was well exposed to sun in the hot weather.

The Sexton of Kakanadukara church who decorated the tomb with flowers sent by Sabu was wonder struck when he noticed the unwithered flower even after seven days.

"It is nothing but a miracle. No doubt about it." Sexton cried aloud.

He reported the mystery to Vicar of the church. The Vicar personally visited the tomb and affirmed, that the sexton's statement was true. Yes of course, it is a miracle. The flowers did not wither!

The news flashed like wildfire. Not only the parishionerss, people from nearby villages and Ernakulam town rushed to Kakanadukara cemetery to visit the tomb of Enasu, and witness the miracle.

"Enasu was a deity". Somebody proclaimed, so many repeated.

"I personally observed it every day. I am the one who decorated the tomb with these flowers. The flowers were exposed to sun for seven days. Look there is no withering. The flowers are intact and fresh. The Godly Spirit of Enasu has maintained its freshness. It is a Godly sign." The Sexton explained to the people who visited the tomb.

The news about the un-withered flowers on Enasu's tomb had reached the Bishop. He sent his representative for verification and ascertained that it was true!

As requested by sexton, with the permission of Vicar, Sabu had erected a beautiful Canopy with Fiberglass over the tomb of Enasu. People started to lit candles on the tomb. Some ladies started to recite Rosary at the tomb. Somebody said to have had a miracle cure from fever. Somebody said that, he was relieved from migraine. The rumors spread widely.

That was the time Kakanadukara church was facing acute financial problems. The church parish committee found it very difficult to raise funds for the renovation of the church. Repeated requests made by the Vicar during sermon to give donation and offerings to church for the renovation was not fruitful.

"Why don't we try to get Enasu Canonized" When the parish council secretary Mathew put up the proposal in the council all members laughed.

"Hey, I am not joking. Nowadays our Pope at Rome is very liberal in canonizing the people. He had already canonized more than eight hundred and fifty people after his resumption as Pope. More than one thousand people were beatified. A huge number of people were declared as "Servant of God" and all those people are on the way for canonization. This is the correct time we push our candidate in the same stream. Once we get a person declared as "Servant of God," we won the game. Our financial crises will go away. We can mint money. In due course of time the "Servant of God". would be proclaimed as "Venerable" then "Beatified: as blessed and would become Saint. It is not at all a bad idea to have a Saint in our Kakanadukara church." Mathew concluded.

"For God sake, Mathew, please don't babble. We are very seriously discussing to find out ways and means to collect some funds for the renovation of our church. Don't divert the discussion to some other subject which is practically impossible." The vicar presiding the council meeting got annoyed.

"Father, I have put forward this suggestion very seriously and earnestly. Please look at the churches that have, a saint or a servant of God with them. They are very rich churches now. One day they were poorer than our church. Now they mint money. We have a very worth and apt person Enasu, to be projected as a candidate for canonization. Enasu was a godly man. He was a deity. That's what people say. Just remember the miracle that had happened at his tomb. For twenty days those flowers were alive and fresh without withering. Now people are coming daily to the tomb and praying. Somebody had received miraculous healings I heard. People started to light candles and recite rosary at the tomb. We can influence Bishop and make Enasu as a "Servant of God" If we would make him an "intercessor of Kakanaduakara," our church will become the richest church of this district. We would be able to renovate the church, we would be able to construct a hospital, and a school under our church. How is it?"

Mathew looked at the Vicar proudly.

"But it is not that easy to get a person Canonized by Vatican." Vicar said. "There are numerous procedures to be adhered to. There will be so many hurdles to face. There must be some sort of an authentic miracle which should happen by Enasu like healing of a severe disease or deformity. Then only the proposal would be accepted." Vicar argued.

In his voice there was an inclination towards Mathew's proposal.

Mathew said "Father if you give a silent approval to go ahead with this programme, we will see to it that, all these would happen. Enasu's son, Sabu will be with us. He is the richest man in this region. Then why should we worry. Everything will be done. All those procedures and the hurdles were made by man and could be overcome by man. This has been done before and would be done in future also, that's what I personally belive".

The meeting unanimously entrusted Mathew to prepare a proposal and a petition to be submitted to bishop to take immediate step to proceed to declare Enasu as a "Servant of God".

Next day onwards more people started to visit Enasu's tomb with flower and candles.

A new, "heavenly Intercessor" was born, "Enasu, Vazakala!"

# Author's note

Devil and Deity is my twentyfifth book and third in English. All the three English books are translations of my own Malayalam novels. Translations are done by myself.

'The Upsurge' was my first English translation, and its original is 'Padayottam', malayalam novel was published by current books (3editions) in 2002, 2006 and 2008.

The second was 'Untold Gospel', translation of my Malayalam novel 'Ariyatha Suvisesham' published in 2010 by H&C publishing House. Both the English books are published by Amazone as e-book and paper back as well, and are available in kindle store along with my other three Malayalam books.

'Devil and Deity' is the English version of my Malayalam novel 'Mithya' published by Kerala Sahithya Mandalam in 2016. I earnestly hope that this book also would be widely accepted by the readers like my previous books.

I assure my readers a good readability.

**V.J Mathews Vanniyamparambil**
**South Kalamassery - 683104**
**Cochin, Kerala**
**Mail id - vj.mathews44@gmail.com**

## Publishers note

### Devil and Deity
### Novel by V.J Mathews, Vanniyamparambil

We are pleased to publish "Devil and Deity" by V.J Mathews Vanniyamparambil who was former Vice President of Kerala Sahithya Mandalam. This is his twenty sixth book and third in English.

Devil and Deity is the English version of his Malayalam novel "Mithya" published by Kerala Sahithya Mandalam in 2015, which enjoyed vide circulation and rated as "a great book with good readability."

Kerala Sahithya Mandalam was established in 1979, dedicated for the promotion of literature activities, founded in 21.01.1979 having Regn. No. EKM/TC/8/2013. Kerala Sahithya Mandalam organizes workshops and seminars regularly, provides research facilities and guidance to writers and poets, publish books and journals and also present Sahithya Awards occasionally.

Kerala Sahithya Mandalam has published fifteen selected books so far, "Devil and Deity" is the sixteenth one.

We are proud to present this great book to the readers.

Cochin
01/12/18

**Kaloor Unnikrishnan**
Vice President
Kerala Sahithya Mandalam
Srikandath road
Ravipuram- Cochin-682016
Ph-9400436347

## Other books published by V.J Mathews

| Title | Publishers |
|---|---|
| Adiyozhukkukal (3) | Current books |
| Vazhithirivukal (2) | Current books |
| Vairudhyangal | Current books |
| Parivarthanam (2) | Current books |
| Nettipattom Kettiya- -Kuzhiyanaakal | Currentbooks /Amazon |
| Sakhsyam | Current books |
| Padayottam (3) | Current books /Amazon |
| Prathikriya | Current books |
| Smrithiradham (2) | H&C |
| Ariyaatha Suvishesam | H&C |
| Pithruvanam | H&C |
| Chuvadukal | H&C |
| Prathigamanam | KSM |
| Babel Gopurangal | KSM |
| Midhya | KSM |
| Pinnampuram | KSM |
| Kazhchappaadu | Author |
| Tharangam | KSM/Amazon |
| O Jerusalem (Screen play) | Author |
| Pithruvanam (Screen play) | Author |
| Vidhi (Screen play) | Author |
| Sthreedhanam (Drama) | Author |
| The Upsurge(English) | Amazon |
| Untold Gospel (English) | Amazon |

www.ingramcontent.com/pod-product-compliance
Lightning Source LLC
Chambersburg PA
CBHW050013170726
48282CB00025B/384
*9789353468224*